About the Author

Dreena Collins has been published online and within collections, including the Bath Flash Fiction Award and Reflex Press anthologies. Her short fiction – and collections – have won numerous awards. She also writes prize-winning, contemporary easy reads (The Hummingbird House series) as Jane Harvey.

Dreena lives in the Channel Isles with her spouse, son, and a naughty dog. She is a social media geek. Find more of her work (and wordy memes and quotes) at any of the following:

http://dreenawriting.co.uk
www.facebook.com/dreenawriting
www.instagram.com/dreenawriting

Collected (Two)
The Complete Stories Vol. II

Dreena Collins

ISBN: 978-1-7396126-9-6

Contents

One

The (Almost Entirely True) Story of Jessie and the Mountain

(First published online by Flashback Fiction, 2020)

Jessie would not go.

They told her that she had to move. The mountain, *y mynydd*, was sliding ever closer: inching and scuttling shingle and stone until one day it would subside. It was for her own good, they said. Her safety.

She stood in her porch, looked up towards the peak, mottled in purples, greys, greens. They talked as if it was sly, this crag. Not to be trusted. And it was steep and splintered, sharp — but it was a confident landscape. Reassuring.

These men did not worry her. She had met liars before.

She was *dewr*, she was cynical. 18 cats at her feet.

A hundred residents had already left, or more. The men were quick to knock down what they could. Of the few houses left, most were abandoned and hollow; the remains of the terrace had slipped into disarray. Doors and windows boarded or broken - casements gaping into black rooms like a row of rotten teeth.

Jessie kept her steps swept; her windows clean.

She invited politicians to see; made them cups of tea - *cryf* it was. Strong. They did not expect her, pinnied and rollered; they did not expect her 75 years. They sat in her kitchen, discussed mountains and valleys, values.

The council gave an order: it was illegal to stay. But she was not concerned. 23 cats at her feet, she rarely left her home now. She was no fool: they would come as soon as she was absent. They would come for her cats and her home and her memories.

The gaps in the street turned to furrows, edging closer to her door. There was less between her and the mountain, each week, and the scene of the summit from her doorway grew broader, encompassing the view.

Jessie was powerful – *pwerus* - but she would not have called it such. She was just staying home, she said. She only wanted to be left alone.

'But what about the mountain?' they asked. Surely she was fearful?

But no, no matter, it would not shift. Mountains hold steady and true. Mountains do not lie.

Inching, crawling, day by day, the vehicles crept until they were at her front door. The only door left. The street was a battlefield: they were caked in mud and purpose.

Jessie stood in her porch; 26 cats at her feet. The men came to her, equipped and armoured, ready to go - but she was not. She looked to the mountain, its purple, grey crest: 3000 feet high. 30 million years old.

He was laughing, the one with the hat, a smugness to his face as he explained – very slowly – why she really did need to leave.

Jessie took a swig of tea. *Cryf.*

And as he spoke, she filled the porch, the space wobbled and shuddered - until she was a *draig*, until she was *y mynydd*. All encompassing. *Dewr.*

29 cats. Determination. Truth. That was all it took.

Because mountains do not move.

Based on the true story of Jessie Moore, who, along with the residents of eleven other households, refused to leave her home in Troedrhiwgwair mining village (South Wales) when ordered to do so during the 1980s. She remained in her home for the rest of her life. Her house still stands.

Two

The Mermaid's Tale

(Longlisted in the Fractured Lit Fractured Fairy-tale Competition, 2021)

On Sundays, he fills the bath with warm water.

I yearn for tepid brine; brackish oceans. But he does not know this. Because he has never asked.

Around us, they crowd and crane. The best seats are raised above; he has constructed a bridge arching over my stage. Those with power and influence can view me there, in comfort. Elevated. And yet they are all the same wherever they sit; slack-jawed, teeth exposed, like Angler Fish, or Bass. Gawping. Gulping.

Beside me, he smiles. One hand on my shoulder, the other on the tap. He is proud, and he loves me. He loves me. He loves me. I know.

I grab the sides of the bath and bear down. I envision my journey as I dive and coil and slip through the sea, bursting through water, piercing, rupturing the surface amidst dark blue peaks and troughs.

And it is over.

My skin has dissolved into scales, pulsing, unfolding, blooming as a conifer cone. My toes arrogantly smeared into the twin curls of a tail.

To the side, amongst the masses, a man bursts through and reaches out, touches the tip of me - sardonic eye contact, wet mouth. I shriek, flounder, almost falling from the bath.

"No!"

This is too much. Splashing. Flailing. Screams. I morph again, into another, into something else: a banshee of sorts, or a siren, perhaps, with my whirligig shrieks, thrashes.

They are fascinated, captivated by the horror.

He sends them away then – the show is over. We have all had enough.

Later, dried, four-limbed, alone, he asks why it had bothered me so. The man was just curious. A curious fool.

I tell him: "I miss my home, that is all. I miss the dark. The deep. The sea."

He frowns, pauses, "But here you are safe. Adored, admired. That is all that was."

"Yes, I am safe. But no, that was not adulation. That was not respect."

"Respect?" He laughs. "What an odd thing you are."

"But why should I not want for what I had before? How should I not crave liquid, shale?" I cry, as he staggers back, a little, made unsteady by my words. "When I was a girl, I was one of many. I miss those days."

He stares.

"You are a mystery to me," is all he says.

He shakes his head, amusement, disappointment both curling his mouth. Mystery is not always a good thing, it seems, and so we climb into bed silently. Within moments, he sleeps; the gentle hum of his breath vibrates the air; the heaviness of his body burying into the mattress. He is a snow angel in the sheets.

I flutter my legs out from the blankets and cover my face with my pillow, seeking dark, seeking other worlds. I picture the floor of the ocean, cool and cushioned, shells alive and dead, speckling the silt, my feet indenting, prints and then toes melting into nature.

And I am there. Poor. Common. Diving amongst seals and kelp; shoals of fish tearing through opaque, heavy water like bats from a cave, curving and weaving above me in an arch. A bridge.

And not one of them – not a single one – gives me a second glance.

Three
Little Squares
(Highly Commended, Flash 500 Competition, 2020)

My mattress is pushed up against the wall. I'm in the corner of the basement where there was once a sink. One pipe remains, lilting away from the plaster. There are tiles, still, lime green - dated. When I lie on my mattress, I face the wall and gaze at them, imagining the moss that grows in the grout as hedgerows, the tiles as fields seen from the sky.

Little squares.

I picture myself flying above them: the wind on my face, hard and cold and real.

Luiza tells me that our debt will be repaid soon. It must be. She rubs my back while I face the tiles, tells me how she will go back to her mother, her sister, her baby, the very day they give us back our passports. She will not be returning with savings, but they will understand, she says. And she will not tell them about this: the basement, the club, the rooms above. She will not tell them about the work.

I do not think they will understand. But I say nothing.

I pull my blanket around myself; the only possession I have. I claimed it the first month I arrived, comforted by the patchwork squares, reassured by the colours. Ana had it first, but she left one day, had not returned.

In the afternoon, I watch the clock on the shelf above the washing machine. The batteries are failing, and days take longer to wind around; the time when Dan appears is different each day, the clock says, though this is unlikely. It is true that he has been known to come in the afternoon, sometimes, and once at dawn. But usually, it is the evening.

We stay here alone for most of the day. We do not exist when we are not with them.

I watch the hands of the clock scissor to six-thirty; I feel my skin stretch tighter across my muscles, bones; the string of my tendons twitching in my hands.

Then a rush of noise, thuds, bellowing cuts the air. Furious, urgent. Panic. Fast.

I hear Dan's voice call to us, yell, though he doesn't appear. He tells us to get out, leave, out, now. NOW.

A raid. Police.

'We must go,' Luiza says. 'We must go now,' she says, as she grabs my shoulder, jerks me back and forth. Her eyes are alive.

'Why?' I ask.

'We are breaking the law,' she pleads. She says it with the same inflexion Dan uses. 'They will throw us in jail.'

'No,' I say. 'No.' I turn away.

I watch her run to the stairs, scrambling, slipping, too late, as two figures appear at the top.

I pull my blanket up above me, arms outstretched, waving. I find a little white square to raise front and centre to signal my surrender: please. See me.

And then I feel it, the hint of a new wind across my face - hard and cold and real – as they enter the basement.

Four

Still Blue

When the nurse comes into the room, I jerk my eyes open. The lids are heavy and swollen, and my eyeballs gritty and dry. Sandbags. But I don't like it when people are in my room when I'm asleep. Luckily, I can sense it these days. Even when they are quiet.

It's a mundane superpower, but you'd be surprised how handy it can be.

She comes around to my right side, and I am grateful. My vision is still blurred to the left. When Doctor Harman did her rounds this morning, I felt nauseous by the time she left, having to turn my head towards her and squint through ripples – though I didn't say anything.

"How's the pain?" she asks, absent-mindedly tucking in a bedsheet.

"Not too bad, thank you," I answer politely, my voice thick and sticky.

I have always hated lies.

She checks my cannula and the drip and then writes something on the notes at the foot of my bed. She turns to leave again. I listen to the dull squidge of her shoes on the floor tiles; wait for the stale breeze that slips into my room each time the door is opened.

"When will I be able to go home?" I ask.

She pauses and does a sort of half-smile that is at once both sincere and patronising.

"It'll be a couple of days yet," she says. "We need your pain under control, and you've had quite a serious operation. There's no rush."

She walks towards the door but pauses halfway there, and then twists back towards me, swiftly, on one foot. Even in those ugly shoes. She could be a dancer.

"You are safe here, you know. I mean, it's our job to look after you."

It's an awkward speech, clumsily delivered, and I appreciate the intent.

But I have always hated lies.

***

Mum's back the next morning, bang on the dot of visiting time. I asked them to sit me up and change my nightdress. I don't want to see the shock on her face again. I don't want to have to worry about her. And the whole thing is so bloody humiliating.

"I bought you some juice and the *things* you wanted."

She says 'things' in a whisper so low and scratchy she is forced to clear her throat afterwards. I can taste the gravel of it in my mouth. She means sanitary towels. It strikes me as bizarre that she is too uncomfortable to say the words, and yet the nurses who have wiped me and placed their thick, cotton towels between my legs have shown no such embarrassment. They have swaddled and mopped me. And I have been too weary to care.

"Thanks!" I say, in a voice that I had intended to be bright. Instead, it is filled with helium and caffeine.

She sits, takes my hand, but looks at the floor.

I glance down and see the back of her hand with its tea-stained skin, pale, covered with a map of blue veins. Her wedding ring rolls to one side, loose. It looks almost tired.

"He's still in there, I hear. Jennifer saw his father at church. She said he looked awful."

She means Adam.

"Right," I say, pulling my hand out from hers. I scratch my other arm to disguise the movement, grating the dry skin into dandruff and scales, noting that the row of little circles that form a constellation on my arm are changing, the bruises shifting from blue to brown.

"Intensive Care, I mean."

"Yes," I answer.

"I just thought you'd want to know."

"Yes." This time, it is louder. Too loud.

"You still don't want to see him, I take it? They said they could arrange something. It could be a good idea, in case, well…"

I shake my head once in a tight, sharp movement. I notice my hair, greasy, cold, as flaps against my forehead; the pain in my neck from that one simple action.

She sits for a while, says nothing. Then she pulls a newspaper from a plastic bag, resting the sheets against my leg as she turns the pages. They are light, of course, but I can still feel them. I sit and absorb the sound of the paper, footsteps up and down the corridor, breath, heavy, grating beside me.

I close my eyes. But I don't sleep.

After a while, a nurse strides into the room, pushing a trolley. I don't recognise her.

"Are we all O.K. in here?" she calls cheerily as she swaps my empty water jug for a full one.

A sudden sob rips from my mum, and the newspaper falls to the floor; she has both hands to her face, fingertips digging into eyeballs, head twitching back and forth, wet chin. The nurse is shocked; I am not. She comes to her side, pulls one hand down forcibly, compelling her to make eye contact.

"Hey! Hey! Come on!" she says. "Everything is alright. She's alright…. Maybe you should go home, get some rest. It would,+ be better for both of you. You are no use to her exhausted."

She is rubbing my mum's shoulders. I can't recall a time when anyone has ever done that to her. I don't like it.

My mum moves to half-stand, but not to leave.

"I just don't understand!" she cries. "And you tell me nothing. You give me nothing. How am I supposed to make sense of this?"

I turn my head to look straight ahead, then I close my eyes. But I don't sleep.

"Just tell me! Tell me what happened. Please."

"I've already told you," I say. Eyes still shut.

"You've told me bugger all," she says. My mum never swears.

I hear the noise as she gathers up her things: the plastic bag, rustling like undergrowth, its objects shifting and rustling inside; the screech of the chair on the cheap linoleum; the muttering of the nurse as she flits around her.

"Well?" she says. I can hear that she is at the foot of my bed. I open my eyes, I make myself do it, and try to rest my face in a neutral position. Sincere. Perhaps a little patronising.

"We were driving along, and a cat darted in front of the car. I swerved to avoid it. There must have been oil on the road, or water, or something. I skidded into the barriers. There was nothing I could do."

She makes a noise in her throat. I can almost feel it in my own. Like bile. And she walks off.

***

The next morning, my headache has returned, but I say nothing to the nurse. In fact, I say nothing at all. It's better than lying.

Dr Harman comes to see me slightly earlier than usual. She is with the same nurse from yesterday. This time, she sits down.

"Jayne tells me your mum was quite upset yesterday."

I nod.

"And that you have been quiet ever since." She doesn't wait for my response. "You don't have to have any visitors, you know. It's not compulsory. It's up to you."

I look at her, surprised. Unsure what to say.

"She keeps asking me about the crash," I say. "I don't want to talk about it." My voice sounds feeble, grey.

"We're here for you. No one else. I want you to get better and to feel safe here," she pauses. "And to be safe when you leave."

I turn my face up towards hers but focus on a spot to the left of her nose, just below her eyeline. I wonder if she notices. I wonder what she knows.

"Thank you," I answer.

She sighs and then stands, pushing herself to a standing position with the arms of the chair; then she moves towards me and leans in. For a moment, I think she will hug me. Then she reaches her hand out, and her long, slim fingers gently touch the bruise that circles my neck. Still blue.

***

Mum doesn't appear at visiting time, and I wonder if they turned her away. But then Inspector Johnson arrives, and I think this could be some pincer movement where she has sent him to ask me the same questions. The same questions he has asked me twice before. Again.

He sits, pulls the chair closer to the bed by grabbing the plastic seat between his legs and making an awkward shuffle. He tries to create some sort of bubble of intimacy by resting his elbows on the edge of the bed, then thinks better of it when he realises the height is wrong. I watch as he lifts them up, and down, props them on the arms of the chair, then eventually places them together in his lap in an awkward prayer.

"I have some news. Some serious news, I'm afraid." He drops his eyes to his hands.

I feel the pump of my heart jammed into my throat, pulsing. Choking.

"Last night, Adam Walmsley suffered a cardiac arrest, from which he did not regain consciousness. The team did their best, but they could not bring him back. He's gone."

I can smell his aftershave, severe and crisp and artificial. My throat constricts, tighter still. Tighter. Involuntarily, I feel my hands rising to my neck. There's a noise. Is it my noise? There's a noise, higher and sharper and my throat is tighter and tighter with his smell and my hands and my heart in my throat. My heart is in my throat.

My throat.

***

After that, I tell them what he used to do. I start talking. I cannot stop. And I tell them what he did that day: how he choked me until I thought it was over. I wanted it to be over. But then he dragged me to the car and made me drive.

Sometimes he was silent. Sometimes he was screaming. I don't know which was worse. I don't know how long it lasted. And he punched the side of my face

18

so hard I took both hands from the wheel and saw black, briefly. Then he grabbed the wheel. And we went into the barrier. And now he is dead. I have told them.

I have.

This is true. Every word of this is true. I always tell the truth.

Always.

But I don't tell them the words in between. I don't tell them how I wanted him dead. How I pulled his hands away; pulled the wheel away, swerved the car, me, I did, and I didn't care, I didn't give a shit if I died, too. Right then, I didn't give a shit. I just wanted it to be over. I wanted it to stop. I hated him.

Hated.

I don't tell them. I tell them what they want to hear. And they read it back to me, and I say yes, yes. And then they summarise it all into a soft pink cloud. A soft-focussed version of the truth. And I don't need to say yes again. So, I don't say anything. But nobody seems to care. And then they tell me that it is over. It is over. Over. But no. It's not that simple.

Lies.

Because I still hate to shut my eyes when someone else is in the room. And my bruises will always be blue.

Five
Light Through Bricks

Her hands are strangely pale, he notices. Almost translucent in places. She picks at her nail varnish while she talks. She seems unaware that she's doing it, leaving a splatter of tiny flecks on her skin, some falling to the desk. Like a trail of ants. Or fleas, maybe.

She's finished talking, awaits his response.

He shrugs.

Her hands fall into her lap. The ants disperse.

She talks about *calling his mum*. There's an edge to it. Like she knows. Like the thought of his mum's slurred confusion might activate him. But she only thinks she knows. They all think they know.

She says *he has potential*.

He snorts.

It's like he has put up a solid wall, but sometimes she can see the light poking through the bricks. Can see what is inside.

This makes him wince – but it mutates, swiftly, into a scowl.

She wants him to *change his life*, and *thinks he can do it*, she says. *He doesn't have to go down that path.*

That's a reference to his dad. They all know the story of his dad. Though it's just a story to him, too. He can barely remember the guy.

He shrugs again.

Air escapes from her in a wheeze. She continues, but all he can think about is her milk bottle hands and the fleas and sighs, and his banging headache thumping behind his eyes. She's not so bad really, but she's no use to him. This is all pointless.

Eventually, it's over. As he turns to shut the door of the classroom, he sees her at her desk, hands on her face, hair falling down.

On the way home, he goes into the shop, walks straight to the back - although he knows Old Davey has cameras there, too. He shuffles his hands in his pockets to see what he has. 93p. His blood crackles, and he considers lifting a few things. Davey can afford it, right?

Instead, he grabs a loaf of white bread and walks to the till. Old Davey looks at him, then jerks his head to his right, wordlessly. On the counter sits three loaves of bread, half price. He feels an astringent sting on his face but pauses and gulps down his pride. Then he swaps the loaf for the cheaper one, grabbing a small bar of chocolate, too, now that he'll have the change. His mood lifts up at the thought of it.

The journey home is short, and he wonders what awaits him on arrival.

There. She is still there. Sat on the sofa, as she was when he left. Duvet across her knees; water bottle full; biscuits gone.

"Hi, mum," he says. "Did you take your tablets?"

He bends down and kisses the top of her head, but she doesn't respond, continues to stare at the television.

"Mum, it's freezing." He switches on the heater.

He sits beside her and takes her hand. She looks down at his fingers and then up to his face, and a wisp of recognition flits between them. He grabs onto it. Holds it tight.

She smiles.

"Beans on toast for tea, O.K?"

But she is turning back towards the television, lost again. An acrid smell rests in a fug around her.

"We'll get you showered first. Let me help you up."

She is dutiful, docile, lets him help her unfold and shuffle to her feet. As he holds the top of her trousers to keep her steady, he glances at the broken window frame, notes the ice that forms where putty should be, inside and out, little capillaries fracturing within it as it begins to melt. He sees the fissure around the frame, where the plaster is gone, and the broken bricks are exposed.

The light breaking through.

"I got you some chocolate, mum," he says.

Six

The Wire

The shelf around the tree trunk is only half the length of my foot. I'm unsure how I'm meant to stand - do I hug the tree? Try to balance, somehow?

The harness cuts in my breasts and armpits – the fat of my midriff splays out from beneath in a bulge.

Tree trekking is not designed with middle-aged women in mind.

I stick my fingernails into the wood and feel shards of it crumble around my skin and under my nails. Breadcrumb fragments of bark. I turn my feet to the side. I try to trust the wire. Trust to the wire.

"You won't fall," he had said. "I promise."

I close my eyes as I edge around, and an image of Michael is there. Sneering in disgust. Looking away in the distance as he taps his foot, helmet dangling from his left hand. He was only holding it by two fingers, hooked inside, and yet it was swinging like a pendulum. Or an executive desk toy.

I wanted it to fall.

I am around the other side of the tree now, eyes back open, briefly triumphant, before I realise this is only the first step. I have a long way to go.

"Why the fuck would you think this was a good idea?" He had said. "If I wanted to get uncomfortable and risk my life, we could have just gone for dinner with your friggin' mother."

Then he did a fake yawn to show how casual and relaxed he was and to indicate he hadn't really been planning that punchline ever since we arrived. No. And then he sniggered at his own joke, wet-mouthed and arrogant – I could hear him muttering 'dinner with your mother' over again as I walked away. I knew he'd be shaking his head and chuckling. I left so as not to have to witness it.

I had made it across a sort of gangplank, stretching my arms from one hanging rope to the next to stay upright. That wasn't too hard if you didn't look straight down but slightly ahead, I found. The plank was narrow and mottled, but the centre smoothed by the weight of climbers and fear.

Michael had driven us here in flat, hard silence and saved all his vicissitude for when we were buckling up. For when we were public. And I had kept my eyes on Katie, wondering what she would do, as fearful as she no doubt was that her left sleeve might rise to show the crosshatches underneath.

Scowling, silent, she had gotten ready efficiently. She marched straight off to begin her trek while I was still fumbling with my helmet, unsure if it fit and immediately convinced that I had a peculiar-shaped head.

I watched the back of her, leggings twisting in rolls around her chicken thighs, and her hands, their pale and elegant fingers splayed out to steady herself as she walked swiftly over the bumpy terrain.

Now I was expected to enter a wooden tunnel. I was briefly embarrassed at the thought of my backside in an ungainly crawl but then relieved at the realisation that yes, I could do this. And I wouldn't have to look down. Don't look down.

Michael didn't notice Katie until she was some distance away. Then, "Have fun!" he yelled bitterly behind her.

When she didn't acknowledge him, he turned to me.

"Look at the state of her. She'll never make it. She's a bag of bones. A bag of bitchy bones." He spat.

One of the staff who had been checking my buckles and straps turned to him and simply said: *"Dude!"* then stared for a moment before he continued with his work. Michael snorted. I couldn't look either of them in the face. But the young man patted my shoulder, where there were no straps at all, and then gave it a quick squeeze.

"You won't fall. I promise."

Out the other side, and I notice I have ripped the left leg of my trousers. A wide, shallow graze is visible through the hole, speckled and jewelled. No matter. I have had worse.

I'm over halfway there now. I take a moment to absorb the sounds around me: birds and breeze. I try to experience, if not enjoy, the air on my face, the flush of exertion in my cheeks meaning I am both hot and cold at once. I can smell pine and fresh sweat. I must be fifty feet high now, maybe more. Ahead of me, I can see the small lake splitting through the trees. That's where I'm headed. I can do this.

I am sideways, crabbing my feet along a rope while holding onto a wire above me. I can feel the pull of muscles in my armpit and shoulder, rarely used these days. I can't see Katie anymore. Unlike Michael, I knew her core was fierce and bold, but she had surprised even me. Whether it was two fingers up to her father or to herself, I wasn't sure, but she seemed to have completed the course with confidence and ease.

She is an odd little thing. At once fragile and concrete. No doubt we have made her that way.

I wobble, feel my back arch into a graceless curve, my feet swing forward on the rope, my hands cleave to the wire above. I close my eyes again. Trust to the wire.

I never discussed Katie with Michael anymore. When she was younger, he doted on her. Somehow, he used her to make me feel worse. She was beautiful. She was slim. She was funny. She was clever.

By inference, I was not.

And yet, as she grew older, he became both bored and disgusted by her, with her changing shape and occasional acne. He didn't like her opinions, hated her friends, no longer enjoyed the same jokes. At age twelve, she didn't laugh when he compared her hair to mine – long, healthy as it was. Age thirteen, she frowned when he said he remembered when my waist had been as neat as hers. She didn't giggle. He had never forgiven her for that.

Age fifteen, the first lacerations appeared. At least, that's when I became aware of them. He stopped talking to her almost entirely after that.

I only have one more plank to cross, and then I will be at the zip wire.

Really, it's a wonder we even got as far as arriving here today, let alone that I am completing the circuit. When I first suggested it, Michael hadn't responded at all. Said nothing. But I put it in the calendar on our phones, wrote it on the calendar on the fridge, and printed the tickets, placing them on the mantlepiece. Right underneath the television. Still, he didn't comment, and up to the point when I started brightly trying to chivvy everyone along today, my singsong reminder of what time we had to leave clearly conveying my nerves, I had thought it entirely plausible that he might tell me to 'fuck off' and pick up the remote control. But he hadn't.

Briefly, I had been pleased. Uplifted. Wondered if we might, for once, experience the kind of day that other families seemed to have so often. Do the things that other people did.

But no. Now I realised that he had only come along to humiliate me and with an even greater desire to see me humiliate myself.

I am there now. Almost there. I close my eyes, and it isn't Michael I see. It's Katie.

There is a member of staff here, clipping me on, explaining how to drop down and step forward in a way so as not to jar myself.

"You'll be fine," he tells me. "Once you've made the first step."

I don't hesitate. I don't look down. I move forward, and I am soaring, not falling. I am flying. Racing over mud and moss and paths and then dark, deep water. The lake. Racing with the wind on my face; cold. Racing with my blood in my ears. And then I can see her. I see her ahead. Jumping up and down with one fist in the air. Screaming, screaming for me. Exhilarated. Strong.

She is tied to me as by a single, unbreakable wire.

"Go, mum! Mum! Mum! You fucking star!"

Her sleeve is riding up, revealing the dark red lithograph beneath.

And I know what I have to do.

Seven

From Poppyseed to Pumpkin
(First published online by 101 Words in 2020)

The first time, you were my little seed. Five weeks old. Just a sesame, they said. I knew you were much more.

From poppyseed to blueberry to kidney bean, that autumn you made it through a riot of shapes and colours. I laced a nest of fingers around my belly; thought I kept you safe.

I was wrong.

This time, I stay as still as you allow. I curl into a ball, bedbound, and count the minutes, hours. A knot of prayers inside my hands.

My little mango, twenty-three weeks. Sweet. Plump. Almost ripe. Almost.

I need you to reach twenty-four.

Six Statistics

1. Up to 30 million people are believed to be victims of modern slavery worldwide. *The World Counts, 2021*.
2. There were 17,616 offences of coercive control recorded by the U.K. police in the year ending March 2019. *Women's Aid, 2019*
3. At least 178,000 under 18s were carers in the U.K in 2019. *Carers U.K., August 2019*
4. In 2009, the Israeli government issued a $1 million reward for anyone who could provide proof of a mermaid said to have been spotted by dozens of onlookers on Kiryat Yam beach.
5. 1 in 50 women experience two or more miscarriages. *The Lancet, 2021*.
6. And Jessie Moore (75) really did have 29 cats.

Eight

Embers

Shortlisted in the Retreat West Quarterly Flash Competition, 2021.

We are three shades of red. Auburn, copper, sand. Dutifully, we tilt our heads together for the photograph – my sisters leaning in, their long hair falling around my shoulders until we become one tangled mass. Mum is delighted at the sight of their thick manes, disguising my short crop. Susie rests a strand of hair over my head, her cheek pressing hard against mine.

Her hair is closest in colour to dad's. She is a reprint of him, but softer. An echo. It's their turn now, and she laughs when Dad suggests she sit on his knee. Eventually, they stand back-to-back, arms folded, propping one another up. Their hair is burnished, metallic. Elizabethan fire.

He kisses her forehead after Mum takes the picture and then runs back to the barbeque, turning the last few pieces of meat over the dying heat.

Then Susie and Jennifer are together. Jennifer suggests they sit on the rug. Somehow, they know how to pose, how to languish and lounge and laugh in a freeze-frame. There are only eighteen months between them. I am the youngest. The accident.

They ask me to take a picture so that mum can join them. She says no, she couldn't possibly, but it is a half-hearted protest; she is holding her phone out towards me as she says it. I struggle to reach it but say nothing. They sit together, her central, black hair now streaked with grey, skin darker than theirs, jaw stronger - but their three mouths the same. Three perfect smiles grin in unison as I fumble with the button.

Jennifer, still smiling, gets up, takes the phone, and asks me to join them. She comes behind my chair and pushes me over the unforgiving grass. She doesn't wait for my answer: leaves me, planted, behind their stage. She stretches her slender arm up, and out, asks me to duck my head down. But she struggles, and the picture captures only the top of their faces and the bottom of my chin. Briefly, there is a discussion about getting me out of the wheelchair, but this is quickly dismissed as impractical.

Dad says the last of the food is ready, calls us his 'little piggies', snorting. Susie leaps forward and squeezes his torso, tells him he's the porky one. There is a little tussle and tickle, a few nips, and pinches amidst laughter. Dad uses his tongs like lobster claws. She flips up his t-shirt, then breaks away – and they are off. Running, racing across the grass. Mum gasps, giggles, grabs a bottle of water, squeezes it at him as he zips past. Then she and Jennifer are running, too. They are running. Leaping. Laughing.

The discarded meat is turning to charcoal on the rusted embers.

I push my wheels in the mud, calling out, but my words are lost on the wind, my tyres wedged in the ground.

So I watch them, in the distance, as they soar like red kites across the grass.

Nine

The Pen

Each time he hurled his insults, Kelly got a new tattoo.

A butterfly when he called her a bitch. A poppy for a pig.

She always had them on her belly: a silent, delicious secret.

Initially, she would go once every month or two. A slag. A slut. A small black swan. She always saw the same man; looked forward to her visits. Trusted him, in spite of his frown.

"Paint me beautiful," she said. And he understood.

Her tattooist listened as she spoke. He would sketch glass-winged butterflies; stratocumulus clouds. He inked her frame, tangling hydrangeas and vines wordlessly. They curled around the lumps of her, unfurled across her skin. And she felt a bit bolder each time she left. She felt more like herself.

But as time went on, she had to pick her battles – raise her game. There were too many skirmishes, too little space. Only four-letter words would leave their mark, now, and nothing said with a laugh or a smile.

Of course, him at home, he never knew. At night, if ever he wanted his way, she kept her vest on, and he didn't complain. His rutting was always hurried; eyes squeezed tight in a wince.

Ironic to comment on her body so much when he never took the time to look, she told her artist, friend, as he chiselled away.

So, he didn't see that she was morphing, winged: etched in dragons and birds. He didn't see that she smiled sometimes. That she no longer recoiled at his words. Her belly still pillowed over the top of her jeans, but she was glad of it these days, pummelled and stroked by her tattooing man.

Eventually, she had to admit that there was no room left. It was over. This would be the last tattoo.

"You choose," she told her sculptor. "You choose me something small but strong."

"I'll paint you, beautiful," he said.

And he did: a tiny wave of letters curling and undulating through the gaps and furrows. Delicate black dots like an army of ants.

Kelly, he wrote again and again.
Kelly. Kelly. Kelly.

Ten

Not So Useless After All

Richard,

Do you remember when I said I was going to take up gardening and you said I was too bloody thick and then you did your yellow phlegmy laugh but this time I ignored you so that made you mad and your face went crinkled yet somehow bloated but you wouldn't admit how furious you were (as that would mean I'd won) so then you were livid because actually the plants grew well so naturally you said my flowers were pointless with a glob of mucus and a twitch and I couldn't understand because they looked like spots of joy and astounded me each morning when their leaves shivered with the weight of dew and promises of the sun yet even though I disagreed I wanted to avoid a row so started planting vegetables too but you hated the vegetables I liked and pretended to gag and puke like a Pantomime Dame while laughing at my purple carrots and refusing them even when they were in a cake a cake a bloody cake and you love cake but you wouldn't even try it so eventually I planted things you liked because I sort of buckled under with your bulk and you ate them just because I didn't say they were mine (ha ha) and I watched and although I am useless and not full of promises and joy like dew and sunshine I had an idea which meant that the next time I cooked I added the worthless flowers Lily-of-the-Valley and Foxgloves and other things you shouldn't eat but honestly you had no idea and then afterwards I buried the remains with the stems and phlegm and puke and then I sprinkled seeds like the babies you never wanted and no one would ever know how bloody clever I was even you you you but I smile anyway while I eat my cake and I watch them sprout because I think I've proved that flowers aren't so useless after all.

Haven't I, Richard?

xxx

Eleven
The Bride

Here comes the bride.

Dutifully, they stood and craned back to see her entrance. She ignored the congregation, eyes fixed upon the groom. A crowd of bridesmaids tottered around her feet in pinks, yellows, peach. They were a falling mound of macarons.

Debbie twisted her own ring, allowed the light to catch the stone, allowed Ben to hold her other hand. He gripped too tightly, thumb rhythmically brushing back and forth against her hand. His skin was dry. His palm was hot.

Doesn't she look lovely?

They all agreed. Her hair was pinned and scaffolded; dress long and tight. Debbie couldn't imagine ever looking that way: felt claustrophobic, constricted simply by watching her. Her breath caught tight in her gullet; it felt trapped and rough, like a baby's cough. She cleared her throat, swallowed hard, but it remained.

41

And they couldn't resist – the others – everyone nudging Ben with a wink and a smile, commenting how he'd be next.

I think I'd like to wait a while.

She whispered it to Tracy, the first time she'd shared the thought out loud. Tracy opened her eyes wide, too wide, but then nodded and said she could do what she wanted, of course. There was no rush. She must do whatever would make her feel happy.

They went through to the reception and the atmosphere shifted: bubbles and snacks and music taking the place of granite and vows. The volume rose around them in a swell, and there was laughter, joy. But Debbie felt tense, Ben holding her hand as if she were tethered to him. As if she might run away. Run away. She hated it but needed it, legs jittering and restless in her too-tight shoes.

Debbie said she isn't sure when she's going to marry Ben, you know.

Tracy whispered it to Sandra, who whispered it to Steve. A little ripple in the room, a frisson amongst the chatter.

They sat; they ate. Ben made small talk with someone's childhood friend; Debbie grinned and nodded at a Godparent and two cousins. And by the time they raised a glass to toast the bridesmaids, her words had been moulded, chiselled, painted red across the room.

Debbie said she isn't sure she wants to marry Ben, you know.

Nine o'clock, and people slowly peeled away from the tables to the dance floor. She wondered when she was allowed to leave. She wondered if she had to stay to wave the happy couple off into the night. A bowling ball in her belly. A baby cough in her throat. Trembling legs. She sat, still. Alone.

Ben was off by the bar, talking, guffawing, when the tittle-tattle came his way.

And she saw him, how he shut down from open to closed – folded in. He looked back at her, aghast, and then he leaned in as they repeated the words, twisted the words, and she knew what they said. She guessed what they said. A choking vine from them to him.

Until he was back. Pale. Still.

Do you want to split up? he asked.

I do, I do, was all she said in reply.

Twelve

Personal Effects

Up in the attic, amid spiders and dreams, I am unsure where to start. Sorting through everything seems an insurmountable task.

I totter on the beams, toddler-legged and careful, as Dad had always instructed. The floorboards weren't strong enough, he said. And I do as I'm told. Always.

No use putting this off any longer.

The place is orderly but caked in snowdrifts of filth. I turn to the suitcases on my left; pull the brown leather one towards me, disturbing a dusty moth.

"Sorry."

Mum always taught me to apologise, and now I say sorry like a reflex. Like a tic. To people; to animals; to inanimate objects. Dead insects. Fifty, one hundred times a day.

Sorry. Sorry. Sorry.

The clasps resist opening, rusted, stiff. Inside, I'm met with photo albums and loose pictures - cascading across one another, jumbled, faded. I move the albums aside, then bundle the loose images up. Mum's face is duplicated in various shades, over again - Dad behind the lens. Her, the same, yet different. Ageing, bloating, shrinking over time. She is unsmiling. I allow the photos to tumble, one then another, swiftly, flowing, a waterfall of criticism and memories. I see her, staring, chastising, again and again.

Then I take a bin bag and shovel them in.

Ten minutes later, nothing but a neat stack of albums remains. Jack can have those.

I am lighter. I feel different.

I move on to the next case. I can feel the tips of my fingers slippery and thick with dirt. Its clasps are fiercely sprung, and fire open with a crack. A silverfish flits into the creases of the fabric inside. I do not apologise.

Ha. That's odd.

There is a Christening Gown: browning, crisp. It's the gown Jack wears in the picture on the sideboard. The same one worn by our father before him. I wonder, vaguely, what I wore to my Baptism - where those images are.

Jack would probably want this, I suspect. He has strong feelings on what to keep and what to throw – though not so strong that they extend to helping me. It's not gracious to think this – I know it – but for once, I don't care. He isn't here, after all.

I hold it up – a tangle of impractical ribbons and lace. There is a small stain across the crumpled silk. I probably did that. I rub at it, scratching with my finger on the artificial nap. The weave starts to drift apart. I rub harder until it splits.

"I do apologise," I hear myself say, heavy with sarcasm.

Huh.

It is ugly, it strikes me. And damaged.

I throw it away.

The next suitcase has a zip. It opens with a buzz, smoothly. I am speeding up. In my stride. There are dresses inside – my dresses. Pink. Puffed. Neatly folded and pristine. Fifteen, twenty years old. I suppose I should consider whether Jack wants them for his girls. But no. It does not matter what Jack wants. It doesn't matter.

Hmm. Wait. Does it?

No.

I hated those dresses. Dad thought girls should be seen and not heard; rosy and unreal. I remember the day I carried a worm to him in my petticoats. I was proud of my find – long and leathery. I held it in the fabric as a sling and staggered over. He threw it at the fence – said I was an embarrassment.

I can still picture the crimson blood of the worm, smearing the wood as it slid down.

He would want me to keep them.

I take the dresses and bin them.

Well, well, well.

Three cases down, I am pleased with my handiwork and considering my next steps. My face cracks into a smile, and I begin to think that, yes, I can do this. And none of them are here to stop me, after all.

I can do whatever I want.

Perhaps I would rent a skip. Perhaps I would start a pyre, watch the smoke and secrets disperse in the wind. Flecks. Fumes. Motes. Perhaps I would bury everything, deep, dark, with bare fingers squishing down into the damp earth, not asking, or listening to anyone else. Not caring what they think or want. Not an embarrassment anymore.

And definitely not sorry.

Thirteen

Adam's Interview

As they waited for the lift, he took in his surroundings. Modern. Clean lines. Bright. And people nodded politely as they passed, he noticed. Nice.

A deferential place.

And good taste too, employing skirt like this secretary. She was fortyish, dressed in trousers… but still… there's no disguising cracking tits and a taut ass.

He could get used to this.

The lift doors opened, and they stepped inside. He watched as she pressed the button for the top floor – nails manicured and pale pink, but short and straight. Shame. He stood behind her, took in the view. A welcome distraction.

"What's your name again?" he asked.

She had greeted him at reception and he had been taken aback, expecting the boss, which meant that his well-prepped joke about the local rugby club went to waste. Perhaps he could drop it in later. But of course, he wouldn't meet him. Foolish really. No one with any sense makes their own way down six floors for each candidate.

There was a pause before she answered. A frown. She had a bit of spunk to her, this one. "Jess Hart," she said.

"Miss *Hart*. That rather suits you... So, what's the boss man like? Any tips for me?"

She looked over; momentarily confused.

"You can tell me." He teased.

She didn't respond – eyebrows raised. He winked.

"I should say not," she muttered, eventually.

He chuckled. "Scorpio, right?"

"Pardon?"

"Your star sign... feisty. Strong. A bit of a sting in the tail."

She shuffled. "I can't say I'm into astrology."

He leant in. "But still... Well? I'm right, aren't I?" She looked away, apparently irritated. "I knew it!"

The lift arrived at the top floor, bouncing gently to a standstill.

"Good at reading signs, are you?" she asked. The doors opened. "Straight ahead."

She stood still and gestured for him to leave the lift in front of her.

"Age before beautiful scorpions," he said.

He was still laughing to himself, shaking his head, as he stepped out. Always a good relaxation tool to have a little banter. It had loosened him up.

And then he caught a glimpse of the sign on the office door ahead of them – oak, solid – *Dr Jessica Hart, CEO.*

Fourteen

Eve's Interview

Not a complete disaster. She hadn't totally humiliated herself. Still, they had all but outright told her she didn't have the job.

Her mobile pinged. Ellie: *Hope it went well don't worry I'm fine xxx*

Perhaps it had been a mistake to mention her own child. She hadn't planned to. But before she knew it, the words had fallen out, one after the other, a string of beads, connected, cascading.

She looked around her on the bus. It was rare that she was travelling in rush hour. She had imagined it would be full of men in suits, broadsheet newspapers. But no. It wasn't the 1980s, after all. There were teenagers on mobile phones; there was a young man in a trendy suit, trousers narrow, short; a woman with immaculate makeup in some sort of tunic with a name badge, reading from an ebook; a mother with a pushchair and a cankerous toddler.

Perhaps she would learn to drive. They hadn't asked that, thank God. It was always humiliating to admit that she couldn't do so by her age. People just assumed that you did, she found. Worse, when they found that she didn't, they seemed to infer that she had lost her licence somehow.

But no, the truth was more mundane. She was only nineteen when she had Ellie and hadn't gotten around to it by then. She thought she had all the time in the world. Then, in the following years, the time was never right – she'd have had to pay a babysitter to go for her lessons, so double the cost. And Michael had said it wasn't necessary. She never went far enough on her own for it to be a priority.

Yet how could she travel afar without the means? It all seemed rather chicken and egg, somehow. Not that she would have said so at the time. It wasn't worth it.

She had been pleased even to get an interview. It was good practice, she told Ellie. She had never had a proper interview. Thirty-four, and she'd never made a formal application for a job, even. Though, of course, she had hoped she wouldn't need the practice. That this would be it.

An elderly lady shuffled towards her and sat in the vacant seat beside her. She smiled and nodded. For a brief moment, speculated that she might have fooled this lady – perhaps fooled them all – into thinking she was a proper grown-up, travelling home from work. A citizen, contributing to society. Making a difference. Or just bloody doing something outside the house, for once.

Just as the internet had predicted, the interview had opened with them asking her about her career to date. She could see they had circled and highlighted things on her C.V. She had talked it all up, as much as she could. But still struggled to think of things to say. There are only so many words you can use to explain that you've been a stay-at-home mum and done some book-keeping and invoicing for your husband for the last fifteen years.

"I see you volunteer for a charity. Why don't you tell us a little about that?" they had prompted.

She felt like a fraud, discussing it, and briefly wondered why she had even put that on the C.V. But the recruitment agency had said it was a good idea to have some different experience. And she did enjoy it, even though Michael had been spitting feathers when she first started.

"Well, I do a lot of it from home. The flexibility suits me. I help with their social media accounts, and I monitor the mailbox, reply to general email queries, forward things on." She was boring herself.

"And what attracted you to this charity in particular?"

This stumped her. What had attracted her? She paused for a moment – thinking she was silent for a beat too long – and that's when she had started talking about Ellie. How proud she was of her grammar school daughter. How she wanted her to have opportunities she hadn't had. How education has the power to transform people, their lives, so this charity, this organisation supporting girls in developing countries, had struck a chord with her.

"I see." The Deputy Head had nodded. "And is that why you want to work for us as a Teaching Assistant? This passion for education?"

She should have said 'yes'. She should have told them that she wanted to build on this experience and give something back. She wanted to do something hands-on. She wanted to make a difference, and she felt that she had the skills to do it.

Instead, she told them she needed part-time hours so she could be home in time for her daughter in the evening.

The bus jolted as it pulled up to a stop, and a little gaggle of young students got off. Four girls, perhaps twelve, thirteen years old. Laughing as they dismounted, sparkly backpacks adorned with keyrings and badges. They were still out, she considered, after five o'clock. Her reasoning for wanting that job was honest – too honest. But perhaps it was ill-founded.

After that, they had asked her some more targeted questions about the role. She was able to answer the ones about job specifics easily – she had spent the last week pouring over articles, researching, and annotating the Job Description. But she floundered when they gave her a scenario about a disruptive child; and drew a blank when they wanted an example of how she had dealt with a difficult conversation. Michael dealt with the customers. She wasn't to be trusted, apparently. And she wasn't sure a difficult conversation with her soon-to-be-ex-husband was the type of example they were after. Though she had a wealth of those.

At the end, as they were about to leave, the Deputy Head had stopped and paused. She asked her why she had applied for this role specifically and why she hadn't gone for the Administrative Assistant role instead. Her experience aligned more closely with that one, it seemed.

"Well, like I said. I want fewer hours than that. I want to get home –"

"For your daughter. Ah, yes. Shame."

In truth, she did not 'want' fewer hours. She needed all the work she could get. Michael had only just moved out two, nearly three weeks ago, but already she was feeling the pinch. And it was very likely to get harder before it got better, knowing him.

Her stop was next, so she pressed the bell and pulled herself upright, smiling as she squeezed by the lady next to her and clutched her new leather attaché bag close to her chest. An impulse purchase – rash, really, as she was unlikely to need it soon.

The stop was close to the house. Convenient. It made it easy for her to travel to work without missing too much time at home, she had told Michael. That was over a year ago now, when she had first been brave enough to broach the idea with him. After he had dismissed the idea of the Open University as a waste of time. He told her she was changing.

Not really changing, though. Just being herself.

As she came in the front door a strong acrid smell of garlic hit her. She could hear the radio in the kitchen, Ellie singing along.

"I'm home!" she called.

"Mum!" She came out of the kitchen into the lounge, tea towel in hand. "I've started dinner. Come and see."

She wondered what sight would greet her, but the place was remarkably orderly. Pasta ready to boil. Bolognese bubbling. Even a salad in a mixing bowl. Ellie grinned.

"I was about to lay the table."

They leaned in to hug each other. "And what have you done with my darling daughter? I should come home late more often."

"I like cooking for you, mum."

She put her bag on a stool and started to unbutton her coat; touched by the scene before her. Tired from the stress of the day. Ellie boiled the kettle and then placed the pasta on to cook.

"How did it go? Was it horrible? I can't believe you did it. I would be wetting myself with nerves."

"I made it to the bathroom, don't worry… It was fine, but it looks like I didn't get it. They told me that they'd be in touch soon as I was the last candidate, and 'if we aren't able to offer you a job on this occasion, please continue to consider us in future'." She made air quotes.

"Oh," Ellie said, frowning. "That's a strange thing to say. What does that mean?"

"Thanks, but no thanks, I think."

Ellie smiled again and gave a small excited jump. "I am so proud of you, Mum, whatever happens. I know that might sound… you know. Weird or something. But I am."

"Thank you, darling. That means a lot."

She put her things away and splashed her face with cool water. Then she went into the dining room and put the placemats and cutlery on the table. Ellie brought the salad in and told her to stop. To sit down and let her wait on her.

Her mobile phone rang. The school.

She had been a good candidate, and they liked her. They really did. But there were others with more direct experience who had just pipped her to the post. As she expected.

"There is some good news, though, if you will consider it. We have struggled to find appropriate candidates for the Admin Assistant role that I mentioned, and we do feel that you would be a very good fit skills-wise and with the team. We would like you to consider this role – I'll send the Job Description through... Now, I know what you said about hours, about you needing to be home for your daughter, but perhaps I could ask you to sleep on it?"

Just then, Ellie walked into the room carrying two bowls of pasta. The sauce smelt deep and rich, and her daughter, her beautiful daughter, tall, independent, grown up, was smiling broadly.

"You know what? Please do send it over. Perhaps I've been too hasty," she said.

Fifteen

Professor Robertson
Sleeps Away from Home

He turned the chair towards the double doors. The light was off, as were his shoes. Coat on his knees; feet propped on an upended bin. This was as comfortable as he would get.

It was surprisingly peaceful in his office. The floor-length curtains had bobbled, thin fabric, and the moonlight shone through, casting irregular shadows. He left a gap to see outside. A single crisp packet danced and shuffled in the breeze. The quadrangle took on a romance and grace that was missing by day.

He felt an urge to burst out, take in the night air. But there were security cameras. He himself had, once, to review a surprisingly clear tape of footage: a student scribing a tirade against the Vice-Chancellor. He recognised the perpetrator but hadn't said so. The VC was an arse.

But who was he to talk?

A fleeting image of Julianna surfaced. Her face when he left. The unanswered calls.

He wondered if the rat would be back. It came along every night. Obese, leisurely, it was a shockingly confident thing. The first time, he thought it grotesque. But then he had started to become fond of it. Familiarity will do that. His eyes searched for it beneath the silver birch tree.

He could relate to that rat. An outsider, not intentionally harmful. And tubby.

Julianna said she didn't care about his weight. But the fact he was changing: his image, his car – this was a red flag. And when he came home drunk, smelling of new aftershave. Evasive. Well, that told her everything she needed to know.

So she thought.

This would never have come about if it wasn't for Pete. With his arrival came laughter, chaos, and too much wine. He had given him the aftershave. Made him think about his clothes. And taken him to that club.

He'd never been to a gay bar before. He wasn't against homosexuality, but he'd always avoided the topic. Gave it a respectful but wide berth. But Pete talked openly, matter of fact, about his sexuality. Frankly, it was refreshing.

Obviously, he didn't fancy Pete. He didn't fancy blokes. Hadn't. But they'd been to that club, and it was heady, hot. Electrifying. Now he didn't know what to think. Because actually, he felt reborn. Like he was starting to see something new: legs of a fawn, blinking awake. Tentative. Scared. Excited. And he couldn't tell Julianna that, could he?

It was late. He needed to rest, and maybe he'd feel differently when the sun rose. The romance of the quad would be punctured by the sharp yells of teenagers, and his curtains would simply look old, worn, tired.

Yet much later, in the morning, when he woke, he found both the moon and the sun were there. The sunrise was partially obscured by the silver birch, with the unyielding moon holding fast and proud beside it in the dawn sky. Together.

And scuttling amongst the leaves, visible, exposed, was his tubby little rat.

Sixteen

Dinner Party

The tagine still smelt peculiar. Even the extra cinnamon had done little to rectify it; Stephanie had hoped it would mask the bitterness. Instead, the whole thing now gave off a stench of hot-cross buns. With tomato chutney.

Bloody Edwin. She knew better than to expect him to shop properly. Even with an itemised list, he always came back with one or two items awry. This time it was no honey ("Whoops! Oh well.") and some sort of peculiar smoked garlic paste instead of a fresh bulb. Apparently, the 'lady in the shop' recommended it. The casserole was already missing the chopped almond its recipe called for due to Edwin's nut allergy. Three ingredients down, she had added Agave and crossed her fingers.

It hadn't worked.

This didn't bode well for the evening, which she was already dreading. It was his idea. They were his colleagues. So how was it that she was stuck in the kitchen, hoping the rather expensive lamb she had used would somehow compensate for other second-rate – or absent – ingredients?

She felt like a child pretending to be a grown-up. And she knew her problems were ludicrous. First world. Petty. Middle-class. But it still rankled.

Edwin wandered into the kitchen, shirtless, for no apparent reason. He smelt of 80s aftershave with a backdrop of body odour. He hadn't bothered to shower. She winced.

He was humming to himself as he opened the cupboard to fetch a wine glass – one that didn't match the set she had already placed on the table – and then grabbed the Chablis from the fridge.

"Can't you lubricate yourself with the Pinot?" she asked. He ignored her and cracked the cap open. "It's already open." She gestured towards the fridge with a knife. He stopped and stared at the blade pointedly. She turned back to the meal.

"Do you want some?" he asked lightly after a beat.

"I bought that one especially." She turned again and made a move to swipe the Chablis from him, half-heartedly. "For the guests."

"I don't believe in keeping things for best."

"That's right. You just do whatever the hell you want, don't you?" she muttered, turning back.

He laughed: deep. Booming. Fake. "Love you too, my darling."

Stephanie glanced at her phone. Seven o'clock. She had thirty minutes, if that, to get ready.

***

61

Twenty minutes later, the doorbell rang. A mist of sweat had settled across her hairline while she had rushed to get ready, cracking and smudging her makeup and curling the little wisps at the nape of her neck. Old. She was getting old.

She had no jewellery on, no tights, no shoes. She called to Edwin to get the door. No response. This would have to do.

It was Annabel, his Assistant. She was a little thing, twenty-five, if that. Stephanie took in the three-inch heels, the sparkling, deep-green dress that flashed beneath her black coat, and the matching eye shadow. She had made an effort.

She was holding a bottle of prosecco, clutching it tightly with both hands. Annabel gave a nervous grin, in a twitchy sort of way, then looked over her left shoulder down the street.

"Ben is just parking the car," she said.

Stephanie realised she hadn't spoken; hadn't even smiled. No wonder the poor girl looked nervous.

"Yes, yes, come in, come in!" She overcompensated, gesturing into the hallway and beaming.

"Well, I'd better wait for him, hadn't I?"

"We will leave the door ajar. He'll find us."

Stephanie reached forward to usher her in and take the wine, which Annabel misread as a hug, leaving them to hopscotch a few awkward steps and air kisses in the doorway.

Edwin and Ben appeared almost simultaneously from behind each of the women as they ended their dance.

"There she is!" Edwin bellowed.

He was wearing a deep pink silk shirt, which clung to his skin in unfortunate places and emphasised the blood vessels in his eyes. Ben wore a soft green jumper with a high neck, matching Annabel's outfit, she realised. The patterned collar of his shirt poked out tastefully. Cotton.

Stephanie took Annabel's coat, wine, and the bunch of lilies that Ben produced. Edwin led the way to the alcohol while she hung the coat under the stairs, then took the gifts into the kitchen.

"I'd best get on with the starters," she called to them as she walked through the lounge. Edwin continued with his story about the sherry he was offering them, leaving Annabel and Ben to nod and smile back and forth between him and Stephanie.

Sherry. For twenty-five-year-olds.

Fifteen minutes later, she was unfettering an avocado from its skin when an athletic-looking woman with short, black hair strode into the kitchen.

"Something smells good," she said. "Can I help?"

She placed a bottle of red wine on the side and started to unbutton her jacket purposefully.

"Oh no, all under control."

"That's a relief." She smiled. "I'm a shocking cook." She leaned against the oven and then jumped back in surprise from the heat, then laughed at herself, pointing at the appliance and shaking her head.

"You must be Rose," Stephanie said. "I would shake hands, but I'm in avocado hell at the moment."

Rose nodded. "Have you got a drink to ease the pain?"

"No, looks like I've missed out on that front."

"Tut, tut. I shall reprimand him."

"You could get the Chablis from the fridge if you like? I'm more than happy to skip the aperitif." She wrinkled her nose. "…Oh, that is, if you are?"

"Sure," Rose said. "In here?" She made her way to the fridge, placing her jacket down on a bar stool as she did so. She was shorter than Stephanie and perhaps five or eight years younger, with tanned, makeup-free skin. She wore a loose, knee-length smock dress and flat, chunky loafers. The edge of a small, black tattoo poked out from under one sleeve. Stephanie breathed a sigh of relief – first impressions of Edwin's new boss were favourable. Perhaps the night would be better than she had feared.

***

They were already three bottles down by the time the tagine came out from the kitchen. Ben had been persuaded to leave his car, which seemed a sensible idea seeing as Edwin had spent much of the previous hour quizzing him about everything from his job to his taste in suits.

"Leave the poor boy alone," cried Stephanie, placing a large bowl of couscous in front of Edwin. "And serve your guests."

"Just making sure that he is good enough for our precious Ani," he replied, picking up the ladle.

A grimace fluttered across his face, and she wondered, again, if he had feelings for Annabel – something she had banished from her thoughts months ago. This was during the period when she was still in shock. Burnt. Wounded. When she had been trying to make sense of his behaviour, unpick his stories to reveal the truth. But the truth didn't involve Annabel. She knew that now.

No doubt his grimace was at the couscous.

She turned back to the tagine and removed the lid of the pot. Ben sat beside her where she stood and tugged her sleeve gently.

"It looks lovely, but I'll have to give it a pass, I'm afraid. I'm a vegetarian." He was apologetic, speaking in hushed tones.

Stephanie dropped the spoon into the casserole dish with a clatter and stared at Edwin, who looked up.

"Steady on, girl," he said.

"I'm so sorry, Ben. I had no idea." Her words were hard little stones that plopped from her mouth. She had asked him. Repeatedly. He had said he would check.

"What's this?" Edwin said, wet mouthed, too loud.

Ben lifted his hands, mea culpa. "It's my fault for being the awkward one. Couscous is fine. Don't worry about me."

"Oh! Never mind. More meat for the rest of us," said Edwin, dishing the semolina onto Ben's plate. "Here, you can have my couscous."

***

Stephanie decided to tune Edwin out and make the most of the company. She managed to settle into conversation with Rose, even though she was sat across from her, and Edwin's strident anecdotes, told to poor Annabel and Ben, overlaid everything they said.

She had been at Johnson and Howe for six months, but various members of the team had been taking it in turns to work from home for at least the first two of those. She was new to the town, new to the company, and was refreshingly candid about how anxious this made her feel. Grateful for Edwin's invitation. It was the first time she'd socialised since a flying visit from her sister two months ago.

Rose looked over to Edwin and smiled softly, and it struck Stephanie that she thought of Edwin as her friend and that he had held this party to be kind.

Kind? Stephanie assumed an ulterior motive. She couldn't imagine him enjoying the company of this confident, modern woman. His first-ever female line manager. He had been quite scathing when she had been appointed, she recalled.

Rose told her about her old role and the differences between that company and this. She talked about a 'toxic environment' and the challenges she had faced while Stephanie picked at her food and topped up their glasses. Stephanie herself had worked at Johnson and Howe until eighteen months earlier. She thought, perhaps, that Rose was still in a honeymoon phase. But she said nothing.

She listened, vaguely detached, while Rose spoke with her decisive, steady tones, and Edwin blared at the others, hardly drawing a breath.

It would have been a pleasant evening without him, she considered. How odd to think that. But it was true.

She picked up her plate and excused herself, started to stack the others' dishes to clear the table. She noted how Annabel's black eyeliner had smudged in the corners and how Ben had loosely placed his arm around the back of her chair, leaning in towards her comfortably.

They had been like that once. For years, in fact. They were the couple who didn't care about public displays of affection. Who held hands as they walked in the streets. Who teased one another and laughed at each other's jokes.

They were in love. Deeply in love. For over two decades. How had it come to this?

She picked up Edwin's plate and looked at him, was about to smile, when he glanced away, eyes glazed, and started a new anecdote.

***

Annabel was talking about wanting children and how multiple births ran in her family. Ben was laughing, pretending to hold his head in his hands in horror, as she described how her second cousin had not one, but two sets of twins. This morphed into a conversation about children's names and whether it was cruel or a matter of personal freedom to give unusual names.

"Thank God we never had to worry about that," Edwin said, raising his glass in a sort of toast.

Stephanie flinched.

Rose caught her eye and asked if she wanted a top-up. She smiled weakly at the woman, nodding her thanks, ashamed as her eyes brimmed.

"I'd best put the pudding in," she said, excusing herself from the table.

She was placing the second bread pudding in the oven when Rose walked in with both their wine glasses.

"You're going to get me drunk," Stephanie said.

"I'm hoping you'll spill all his innermost secrets. Give me the upper hand." She smiled and gave an exaggerated wink. Stephanie took her glass.

"He doesn't have any inner secrets," Stephanie answered flatly. "What you see is what you get."

They both stood still in silence for a moment.

"It's not that we can't have kids. He didn't want them."

"Hey, you don't need to explain anything to me," Rose said, lifting one hand. She took a step backwards.

Was she oversharing? Probably. She didn't care.

"I did. When we met, at least... in the beginning, I secretly wanted them, and I thought he might change his mind. Stupid, really. He didn't. Obviously," she laughed, sardonically. "Anyway, I made a choice. I loved him more than I loved the idea of children."

Rose nodded. Stephanie wondered if she had noticed the past tense.

***

Ben, Rose, and Edwin were all in the garden, smoking. Annabel was talking and slurring, leaning across the table, head resting on one hand. She had plaited her hair and kept trying to tie a knot in it to keep it off her face, but she was failing, and it repeatedly fell down and forward across her forehead as she spoke. Stephanie noticed that she had a new pimple appearing on her chin and that she had lost a false nail, revealing brutally chewed nails beneath, raw and pink.

She was so incredibly young. How had she ever thought Edwin was interested in her? Or, more accurately, she in him? But no, she had been right to. It would be classic Edwin to do something like that. To fall for the pretty secretary. Classic bloody Edwin. And he had been behaving strangely, or differently, at least – and working longer hours. She wasn't totally foolish to wonder if he was having an affair. They were classic signs.

But it was his new boss, ringing the changes, setting higher expectations. That was all. Good for her. And he probably revelled in the opportunity to stay away from home; she could hardly blame him for that.

Ben wandered back in. "Is there something in the oven?" he asked.

"Damn it!" she cried.

***

The bread pudding was finished, and Edwin had insisted on making the coffee. He made a show of it, repeating how she must sit and let him do it. As if she had been declining offers of help all day. But he had made none.

Ben was asking Rose how she found the move – where she had come from and where she grew up. She had moved around a little, she said. She'd been single for years and loved to live alone. She had freedom.

"I don't trust easily. Product of a broken home," she said.

"Aren't we all?" muttered Ben.

"Ah, but I bet your dad didn't have affairs with multiple members of your extended family," Rose countered.

"Hopefully, his wife's cousins rather than his own?" Ben asked.

"Yup. But not just cousins."

Stephanie was taken back to that night three months ago when Edwin had not come home until 3.30 am. Phone switched off. No explanation. That was when it had solidified, this feeling. When she had fallen down into the hole. That was the moment when she could no longer pretend.

"Tell me about Johnson and Howe," Stephanie interrupted. "I'm out of touch. Any gossip?"

"Gossip? Not that I know of. But I could be the wrong person to ask." Rose shuffled in her seat. Perhaps she had overstepped. But she persisted, anyway. Now or never.

"Any new staff? There must be some bright young things there now. I know there have been some retirements."

"Arthur is nice," said Annabel. "And what's-her-name. You know..." she circled one finger in the air, struggling to recall the name. "The gorgeous one."

"Oh, I know. She's called Annabel," said Ben, leaning into her.

"Bethany," said Rose, looking down at the table.

Just then, Edwin came in with a cafetiere of coffee and a carton of milk. No jug. He looked at Rose.

"No more work talk, please," he said. "Who else would like one more cheeky smoke while the coffee brews?"

"I will," said Rose.

***

They were on the brandy and amaretto now, but Stephanie had drunk more than enough, so she had taken herself off to the kitchen. She started to rinse the easiest dishes in the sink to clear some space. The place was a disaster – the thought of greeting the mess with a hangover was enough to spur her on to make a dent in it. Besides, Annabel was talking babies again.

The thought came to her again. That same bitter little thought that she couldn't seem to stop from resurfacing once a week. No, almost once a day. Two decades she had been with this man – she had given him her youth. She had given up her hopes. If she left him now – what was it for? If they broke up, it was too late for her. That time was gone. But not too late for him.

She felt trapped.

Perhaps this was a middle-life crisis. Perhaps this was what that felt like. Perhaps it was her, not him. Hormones. Ageing. Fear. Maybe he was doing nothing – had done nothing, after all.

Rose came into the kitchen again. "Ed is asking if there is more bread pudding."

"Ed?" She had never called him that.

"Shall I just take the dish?" Rose stretched her strong, lean arm out to grab it.

"No," Stephanie turned, soapy glass in hand, "Not that one. That's the pecan one. I made two."

A small, puzzled pinch appeared between Rose's eyebrows. "He doesn't like pecans? The fool!"

"Ha! No. He's terribly allergic. I don't even eat nuts when I'm around him. That's pecan and maple. But we've got a different one, see?" Stephanie gestured to the smaller pan to the right.

"Oh, I didn't know…"

"Don't even share a bed or get too close when I have eaten nuts. Can't even risk a kiss. Not that there's too much of that going on these days." She turned back towards the sink.

Then Annabel wobbled into the kitchen. Her reedy, slushy voice was anxious and high. "There's something wrong with Edwin," she said. "He needs an… an epi-pen?"

Stephanie turned back, a wave of confusion hitting her. Then she caught sight of Rose. She was standing stock still, mouth dropped slightly ajar, eyes wide, unblinking. Looking at Stephanie. Staring. Aghast.

Then the wine glass slipped from her grip, hit the kitchen floor, and shattered into a dozen pieces.

Seventeen

Cashier Number Four

Susan sat down at check-out number four, rearranging the seat height with one hand and grabbing a bottle of sanitiser with the other. She had her routine down. It was a little like starting a car: checking mirrors, changing heater settings, emptying the cash into the till. That sort of thing. She'd been doing this for seven years. The longest-standing check-out staff in the shop.

Not exactly the most prestigious accolade.

Before she'd even started to wipe down the conveyor, shoppers started to close in. Like herring gulls, they were. Beady eyes spotting her straight away. Taking a chance. Hopping closer. Impatient.

She turned on the light above her till and moved the 'Check-out Closed' sign out of the way.

The first customer only had a handful of produce, which he clutched against his chest, both before and after purchase. Not wanting the inconvenience of a basket, or the cost of a bag, presumably. If he could, he'd have had her scanning them in his arms.

He didn't make eye contact; didn't answer her "Have a nice day." It was all over in a few moments.

That wasn't a good start. If he'd been buying more, she'd have been tempted to 'accidentally' scan through one of his expensive goods a couple of times too many. But as it was, he'd have noticed. That only works on the big shops.

The next customer was still laying her goods out, so Susan paused, smiled, held the margarine ready to scan but gave the poor lady a breather. She smiled back at her and nodded her thanks. Susan liked that. Made a mental note to accidentally-on-purpose fail to scan one of the more costly items in her haul.

Next came a young mum. She had a newborn strapped to her chest and a toddler in the trolley seat. At first glance, she looked like she was coping admirably, as the kids had coordinated outfits and expensive shoes. But Susan knew where to look for the signs: nails painted but badly chipped. Coat on the kids, but not on herself. That sort of thing. Her eye makeup was clumpy and smudged: yesterday's, no doubt.

There was a lot of shopping to get through, so Susan switched off and swiped away while her mind drifted. She couldn't stop thinking of the words she'd had with him downstairs this morning. Brian. She could hear the voices as soon as she stepped out of her flat: two, maybe three men. Though by the time she was at the front door, Brian was standing alone on the threshold: spread-eagle like a spiderweb blocking the way. All legs and elbows.

"Fucking Prosecco Poofs!" he was yelling, to the back of a young man who was striding away.

"Excuse me," Susan said.

Brian turned around, wild-eyed.

"Did you hear them last night?" he asked.

"I'm sorry, who?"

"The la-di-dah lads in number one," he spat.

"What do you mean?" Susan asked, genuinely confused.

"Them." He waved vaguely outside. "The boys. Their party. Crap dance music and a flat full of them."

"Ah, no," Susan said, stepping past him. "I'm on the top floor. I didn't hear a thing… but didn't you get their note?"

"Oh yeah." He chuckled, humourlessly. "I got their 'note'."

She turned towards him. "Well then, at least we were warned. It was a wedding party. Can't begrudge them a bit of noise on that occasion."

"A gay wedding isn't a wedding in my book. And giving me a note doesn't mean you've got my blessing."

She turned away; cheeks warm. "Oh well. Live and let live, I say."

"Fucking Prosecco Poofs," he answered.

The young woman's shopping was all scanned, and Susan smiled at her as she loaded the last of her bags back into the trolley. No wedding ring, she noticed.

She couldn't say she really understood it, the way these young people thought. The way they lived. And in truth, it did make her feel a little awkward when she met those young men together in a pair. But they seemed nice enough, and they clearly doted on one another. No harm done. None of her business. Why people had to get so het up about other people's choices, she could never understand.

She was pulled up out of her thoughts by the next customer. He was loading the last of his shopping onto the belt while chewing the ear off someone on his mobile phone. She asked him if he needed any bags, and he waved her away like a fly.

"I tell you. I'm not doing it again. They bloody rearrange this place every two minutes. Stand still long enough, and they'll move the biscuits right in front of your eyes... No. Like hell, it has. It was only two weeks ago I helped you with the shopping. Last month! You must be –"

He came around to the other end to start packing his shopping. Susan continued to bleep things through nonchalantly.

"Oh yeah, that's right, you 'don't feel well'. I'll give something to –" He looked up at Susan briefly and caught her eye. She looked away. "Anyway, I got eggs. You can do egg and chips tonight... what?... Oh, don't be so bloody... You've never said that before. I think I'd remember if you'd told me you didn't like bloody eggs. You're just... Right. Anyway. I've got to go and pack this bloody shopping I've done for you."

He took the phone from his ear and disconnected.

Susan continued to swipe the shopping through, leaving the eggs until last. Finally, she picked the carton up and gave a cursory glance at the eggs inside. As she closed them, she stared vacantly, straight ahead. Then she took her index finger and slid it under the lid, pressing down until she felt a satisfying 'chink' beneath her skin as the eggshell crumbled. She closed the lid and passed them to him.

"That'll be £59.87," she said.

Next came an elderly lady with a basket full of vegetables. She was clutching a purse and frowning. She came in every Sunday, that one. Counted her coins to pay. One time, she even had to put something back. Susan didn't bother her with any chitchat but was careful to make sure that she didn't quite let any of the bags of fruit or veg rest properly on the scales. Just a few ounces off each one. Only a little.

She watched the woman walking out of the shop, keeping an eye because the floor outside was wet. She heard the sound of someone clearing their throat nearby. Looked up.

It was flipping Brian.

He nodded.

Susan started to scan his shopping, and he moved to the end to pack his bags. He was one of those who thinks he is a superior shopper. Had it all worked out. You know the type – makes a big deal out of having a system. Even remembers to bring insulated bags for his frozen goods.

Mind you, there were an awful lot of cheap pizzas and ready meals amongst his things. And alcohol.

"Live and let live," she whispered to herself in an effort to keep her judgement at bay.

Perhaps she said it a little louder than she had intended, as she could have sworn she heard him mutter: "Live and let bloody die."

As she made her way towards the end of the shopping, she noted a bottle of Prosecco amongst the multipacks of own-brand crisps. She paused briefly and snorted involuntarily. She looked up. He stared at her, eyes narrow, daring her to say something, but she took the crisps and scanned them, sliding them down towards him just a little too briskly so that they slid off the side and fell to the floor.

"Oh dear," she said flatly.

He bent down to retrieve them, muttering.

Then she smiled gently to herself and took the bottle of Prosecco in her hands.

Eighteen

Wish. Bone.

Diligently, she gave him the wishbone. Picked clean of meat, of course. She'd once made the mistake of placing it straight onto his plate. Never again.

She had run it under the tap today – water and fingers dislodging gelatinous meat until the fragile bird bones shone in her hand.

Sunday was always roast chicken. Bland, but Jonathan would not hear of lamb or beef. The cost! So chicken it was. Every week for fifteen years.

She dressed the table, as always, staged in a counterfeit domestic bliss. Flowers from the garden. Napkins. Side plates and glasses as identical twins.

He sat.

"What's the veg?"

Jonathan placed the napkin on his lap. She wished he'd tuck it into his front – he inevitably finished with a shirt pocked in gravy.

"Cauliflower and carrots." She poured his wine.

"No peas?"

"No peas."

"Humph," he said.

He drank half his wine in one gulp. She placed his meal down and caught a tiny sneer fluttering across his face. It disappointed her each time. The way his nose wrinkled, lip lifted, caught on a wire.

Then she sat, too.

"There's a new choir starting," she said, leaning to pour his gravy. He raised a hand to stop her, though whether for the gravy or the conversation, she was unsure.

"You're not thinking of joining?"

"Maybe." She wouldn't.

"Oh, I forgot the apple sauce."

She made to stand. It was one of his quirks. Habits. Apple sauce with everything. No matter what.

"Leave it," he said.

"Really?"

She was unsure, perched, hands on the table, ready to launch. He would change his mind. He always wanted sauce.

"Sit," he said. "I want to talk."

She settled, and he began. *Nothing in common now; grown apart; he was bored and sorry, but he didn't find her attractive anymore.*

That's just the way it was.

She watched him push mashed potatoes and gravy and cauliflower against the wishbone she had picked clean for him. She listened, nodded, and felt it fall away.

And all she could think of were the bones that he left – dirty, mangled, used – and how she wished, she wished, she wished he had done this sooner.

Nineteen
The Robin

At the back of the council estate was one corner of greenery. An enormous fig tree arched over from the house next door – constantly pregnant with fruit in shades from khaki to black. But on their side of the wall was a silver birch, which was no competition, as it had never quite seemed to take hold. It was planted in someone's memory – whose, she couldn't recall. The small granite plinth was now devoid of plaque.

But then there was the vast horse chestnut. Her favourite. She had tried, once, to wrap her arms around the trunk but was delighted to find she failed. It must have been over a hundred years old. Two hundred, perhaps, pre-dating the development by some way. She wondered what had been here before the flats to lead to the growth of such a fine tree. Its trunk was squat and twisted as a marshmallow, with branches falling low but strong. Octopus roots dropped sheer into the ground and then burst through the tarmac of the carpark, over a metre away.

It was a confident tree. Wise. And it was where she hid her bird feeders.

Of course, some people must have known they were there. Tucked about the back in the shade, the collection wasn't entirely obscured from view. Besides, she went to re-fill the things every day. She must have been seen.

But you had to be looking – to be staring at the conkers or the loaded fig tree or the tentacles on the ground – before you would notice. And the people who would look for those things, truly look, were not the sort of people who would want to steal a bird feeder.

Sylvie lived on the fourth floor of Block Two: you had to take the stairs; the lift hadn't worked in years. Turn right. Go past the one with all the plastic gnomes and the faint smell of cabbage. Number eleven. She'd been there twenty-six years – 9,554 days, to be precise – and she had fed the birds in her little green corner on every single one.

Today was no different. She carefully peeled the rucksack from her front as she reached the birch tree. She wore it forward, adding bulk to her torso, which was otherwise concave and narrow. She liked to carry it that way. It added ballast, and on her slow journey back home, her newly flattened front reminded her of the good she had done and the food she had shared.

For years, it had been a backpack, of course. Some small part of her pretended this odd sartorial choice was temporary, and perhaps she'd go back to wearing it as it had been designed to be worn someday. But in truth, this would never happen; her arthritic shoulders would not allow her to reach behind her at the angle needed, and she feared the weight, when it was full, might topple her over at the top of the stairs as she descended. The neighbours probably thought she looked daft when they saw her, one hand on the rail, the other patting her bump as she smiled to herself, taking the stairs cautiously and respectfully. She didn't care.

Sylvie rested the bag across her feet. The weight was a comfort, and she had found that she could use her toes to lift the bag, just enough to avoid having to bend over fully to pick it back up again. She put on her rubber gloves. Fuchsia fingered; she was ready.

She started with the suet feeder to break herself in. It was an easy job. It hung from the metal station she had rammed into the earth and was only a slight stretch to reach. It wasn't popular, and the fat block only needed replacing once a week. Only the starlings ate from it, from what she had seen, and even they didn't seem keen. Perhaps it was in the wrong place for them, she wondered, as she wiped away the muck and leftovers before replacing the unit on the hook. But she always had a fear of changing the way she did things, picturing the one loan bird who relied on her coming back to find its food now gone. Its life source vanished.

She couldn't risk it.

She had restocked both the tube feeders with seed when she sensed a presence nearby. A shadow added its weight to the bag, stretching across her feet and pointing towards the horse chestnut tree. She stopped but didn't look. Waited a beat. The shadow remained stock still. So she went back to work.

"What you doin'?"

She didn't turn around. "Feeding the birds."

The question was an odd one, even coming from a child that was, what? Seven? Eight? What sort of answer were they expecting?

"Why?"

There was a pause. Sylvie glanced over her shoulder and watched as the girl cocked her head to one side and placed her hands on her hips – a gesture which reminded Sylvie, unexpectedly, fleetingly, of Peter. She sucked in her breath and did not answer.

The girl seemed to accept the silence, and they both swam in it together for a full minute or two – Sylvie pushing the platform feeder out of its fixing and tipping the leftovers onto the soil while the girl kept her position stubbornly but swayed gently as she watched.

"Where's your coat?" Sylvie asked, the sharp pain in the base of her thumb reminding her of the temperature.

The girl shrugged. The silence swamped them once more until she spoke again, loudly. "They're very greedy."

Sylvie shook her head. "No. Hungry."

"They are." The girl said confidently, with a slight tap of the foot. "I see them."

Sylvie turned to face the girl properly for the first time. Dark-haired, her fringe fell heavily into her eyes. She blinked as it grazed her lashes but didn't move it, and Sylvie had the urge to brush the hair from her face. The girl still had her fists balled up, pushing against her tiny hips. Sylvie could see the tension in her arms and her clavicle poking through her pale skin. She was bold. Sinewy.

"What do you mean?"

The girl jerked her head towards Block Two. "I can see them from my bedroom. After you come over, they go crazy, flapping their wings at each other and scrapping. Sometimes, they even bash into that tree or each other. They go like this."

She lifted her hands and stretched them flat with her fingers so taut that they started to curve. Slap. Slap. She whacked them together to demonstrate the collision.

"Greedy." She nodded her head sagely.

She put her hands back onto her hips but no longer kept her legs locked into the strong V shape they had occupied earlier.

Sylvie placed the feeder on the ground.

"These are wild birds. During the winter, most of their food supply is gone. So the food that people put out for them is important. It's precious."

"Why is it gone? Who takes it?"

"Well, the weather takes it. They eat berries and bugs and things, and at this time of year, there are far fewer of them around. So they fight or rush to eat because they don't know when they'll get any more."

The girl was frowning and leaning forward slightly, listening intently and with vague cynicism as Sylvie went on to explain how fast their metabolisms were, how much time they spent awake, and how they needed to carry weight to fight off the cold. She marvelled at the sight of her and wondered how it was that the child did not know this. Sylvie had no children of her own. She and Peter. They had no children – though not for want of trying. And they almost did. Almost one time. She shook the thought away.

Was this normal? Was this just her age? Or didn't children learn about such things anymore?

The girl dropped her arms by her side.

"So if you don't feed them, they'll die." Her tone was matter-of-fact, and Sylvie didn't know how to interpret her.

"Maybe," was all she said. "Now, I'd better get back to work."

"It's your job?" she asked, bending down to pass the feeder back to Sylvie without comment.

"Ah no… at least it's only a voluntary position." She replaced it in its fixing and carefully poured some food onto the mesh with care. "Could you pass me the peanuts?" she asked.

She may as well take advantage of having a sprightly young thing with her. The girl rummaged in the bag, and for an awful moment, Sylvie wondered whether she might not know what peanuts were. But she waited silently and resisted the urge to bark instructions until she saw a shy smile form as the girl took the nuts from the rucksack and carried them the few steps towards her. She laid the transparent bag across both her palms and held it up regally as she stepped over the curb onto the soil.

"You carried that very carefully," Sylvie observed.

The girl nodded. "You said it was precious," she whispered.

They continued, working in tandem, to fill the last two feeders, Sylvie explaining as she did so about the different species and how they each had various habits and preferences. The goldfinches fought sometimes. The doves came in pairs. Blackbirds fed on the ground. She wasn't lucky enough to have the type of view the girl did, but she watched from afar sometimes. The birds would come if she stayed very still.

"Robins are my favourite," she told her, something she had not said aloud in years. Sylvie was sprinkling dried mealworms onto the ground. "They live in the same place for years. We had one here. But I don't think ours is around anymore."

The girl nodded. "I know robins."

"That's why I put these down. Mealworms. To try to tempt one to make this his territory." Sylvie wondered if she might flinch at the sight of the bugs but was glad to note no change in her.

"Why do you like them?"

Sylvie stood. "They say, 'Robins appear when loved ones are near.' And I find that quite comforting."

"What does that mean?" The girl wrinkled her nose.

The girl was hugging her arms now, the sharp point of each elbow causing tension in her flesh as it stretched across her bones. Her skin was mottled, purple and white, from the cold.

"It means someone who has died is nearby. Someone you loved. Here in spirit."

"Ghosts."

"Sort of. But nothing spooky." Sylvie smiled, wondering if she had overstepped the mark with all this talk of death and starvation. She took off the red woollen scarf she had tucked into the front of her coat and placed it around the girl's shoulders wordlessly. It enveloped her small frame like a shawl. The girl smiled and buried her face into it but did not comment.

"So it's a bit like: worms eat the dead people, then the robin eats the worms, then the robin becomes the dead people."

She was speaking into the fluff of the scarf. Sylvie could almost feel the strange scratch of the wool against her teeth.

"Maybe."

"And then, if you stop feeding them, the robin dies, too! They all die. Dead. Dead. Dead. Gone!" She sounded delighted, slapping her hands together once more, this time to the beat of her own words.

Sylvie stopped. *No,* she wanted to say. *They stay forever. The dead people last forever. There isn't an end. Nothing ends.*

But she simply nodded.

***

For two days, Sylvie had lain in her bed.

The air in her bedroom was thick with sweat and delusions. In between vivid visions of Peter, young and old, she saw her own belly: giant, pregnant and apparently harbouring a nest of chicks. It was real. As real as anything else, she had seen.

She was aware enough to know that she was in her bed, a space she only used at night. Sometimes, she had brief moments of true lucidity. Here, the guilt of her unfed birds weighed heavy on her.

"If you don't feed them, they'll die. They all die," she heard the girl's confident little voice cry out. "Dead. Dead. Dead. Gone!"

This was unheard of. To be sick. Not to feed the birds. But for some reason, her legs were disconnected from her. Loose. Unreliable. It was the most peculiar sensation. She found she could barely get to a sitting position as they weighed her down, tugging her back towards the mattress.

Yet she needed to get up. She needed to get out.

She would have to try.

By the time the ambulance arrived, she had been on the floor for at least three hours, perhaps more. She had no way of knowing.

Dehydrated, they muttered to one another. *Maybe a UTI. Her heart's fine. Blood pressure not ideal, but nothing to cause alarm. Best go for a scan anyway, rule out...* they were talking to one another, not at her, least of all to her, but even then, they couldn't bring themselves to say the word 'stroke', she noted.

After all their testing and prodding, they lifted her onto a stretcher – *a wheelchair wouldn't make the stairs, sweetheart*, they shouted loudly. She wondered if they thought she was deaf or didn't speak English, perhaps. She didn't want to talk, that was all. She was tired and perplexed.

When they came out into the winter sunshine, the sharp blast of cold that hit them took her breath away, and she felt a crackle bubble in the top of her chest. But even with this, she was glad to be outside. It was a beautiful day. The sky above her was bright and clear – a blanket of solid colour. She was happy to feel the air and hear the familiar sounds of the flats mixing with the wind and birds. Gulls, mainly, were what she could hear. But in the distance, she thought she caught a blackbird fighting through the crisp air and car engines.

The ambulance was parked near the entrance at an angle, and for a moment, she was worried it would block her view of the horse chestnut completely. But they took her trolley in a wide loop to straighten it up for the tail-lift of the vehicle. They arced around confidently, clearly knowing from experience the dimensions of the stretcher and the ambulance and the angle required. It was an impressive ballroom dance that needed no verbal instruction between the two paramedics, synchronised and neat. And as they did so, she pushed herself up, balling the fists of her hands and jabbing them hard into the bed.

"Hey, now, Sylvie. Stay where you are," one of the paramedics said. She patted her blanket vaguely.

Sylvie ignored her. Leaning over the side of the trolley, she held onto one of the bars and pulled herself until she had a glimpse of the octopus tree, the birch, the figs. She had a perfect view. She wanted to see if she could spy the feeders. She needed to.

There were no birds. The commotion had scared them away, of course.

But beneath the tree was the lone figure of a young child squatting down in the dirt. She was curled up, scruffy, and awkward. Her slight legs were tucked underneath, pale, bare arms extended, head down. A long fringe grazed her nose.

And she was scattering the ground with something carefully. Sprinkling something precious – as her full red scarf billowed across her chest.

Twenty

Carrie*

August 2022

I know it's dreadful to admit, but I was relieved when that nasty business kicked off about Angie Raynor's legs. For one thing, it means Boris will finally have a second topic of conversation. I can't tell you how sick I am of listening to him blather on about lockdown parties while I'm trying to enjoy my tabouleh.

Smile and nod, Carrie. Smile and nod.

But more importantly, it means he'll be making a big show of late-night meetings with the IPC and whatnot, so I could actually get some peace and a chance to watch *Don't Look Up*. I might even be able to go to that talk on gender identity.

What's that? Oh yes, it's easy enough. Honestly, tie my hair in plaits, dig out my best Birkenstocks, and no one gives me a second glance.

I've probably got a week or two before he'll be away for a bit again. I should try him on Jackfruit in the interim. He was suspicious last time and didn't finish his meal – not like him. But he's been eating Quorn for six months now without batting an eyelid, so I'm sure I can get it by him. I'll add a bit of smoked paprika. Tell him it's pulled pork.

I think I've finally managed to swap out those dreadful Y-fronts, too. I told him the boxers would aid his virility. (Dear God, let's hope that's not true). He doesn't need to know they are made of hemp. I made a big show about how youthful and sexy he looked. Even threw in a few BJ puns.

BJ. Honestly. It's the fact that he actually *chose* the name that rankles the most. He could have stuck with Alexander, but no. He went with Boris because he couldn't resist the oral joke. And then he goes and surrounds himself with blokes named Cummings and Hancock.

Seriously.

Anyway, it's just another few months. I hope. I will admit, I almost gave in last month after he made that disgraceful decision on Rwanda – but then he started talking about lifting the fox hunting ban for a 'bit of PR', and it reminded me of the good I can still do. And frankly, I enjoyed the challenge of talking him around while letting him think it was all his idea. You know how it is.

So, there we are. He'll be tied up, and I could be off the hook shortly after that. The drip, drip-feeding of party stories and incriminating evidence seems to be finally doing the job. Boris has been furious about the whole thing – betrayal, he's called it. I nearly spat out my peppermint tea. Him. Betrayed. Luckily, I covered it up with a little cough and speculated about whether I had COVID. That scared the life out of him.

But if he's still hanging in there in a couple of months, I might have to pull out the big guns.

I've only got one party photo left – but man, it's a zinger.

It probably goes without saying that this is a work of fiction.

For my non-British readers, Carrie Johnson is the third wife of British ex-Prime Minister (Alexander) Boris Johnson. While she is patron of the Conservative Animal Welfare Foundation, as far as I am aware, Carrie is neither a vegan nor a left-wing subversive. (But wouldn't it be glorious if she was?)

Twenty-one

Mid-Life Chrysalis

By the time she was 50, she was an orphan. Can you be an adult orphan? Is that a thing? It should be a thing – distinct, brittle, raw as it is – but they need a better word.

Unicellular.

Or unchaperoned, perhaps.

After this happened, she found herself swathed in it. Nothing was the same. And she walked awkwardly, bundled, stooped, as if she might trip at any time. She was wrapped up in grief.

It was odd, really, how something external could have such a physical effect. Like a calico shroud. And it was almost sheer. But not quite. Not quite. It added weight to her – both real and imagined – and the years sped up like a dynamo.

Shortly after that, she was kicked in the crotch by the menopause. Alarmingly, it did not sneak in during the night, as expected. It did not leave her flushed and dry. Rather, rugby tackled her; it pulsed through her body like a second puberty in reverse. She had the highs, the lows, spots, tears, insomnia, self-doubt, and self-loathing. Even floods of crimson blood between her thighs.

But it was the end of something, not the beginning, it seemed. And she wrapped her loss about herself, hiding behind a cloak of invisibility and dread.

Of course, the end of her youth coincided with the burgeoning of her daughter's. Of course. Her daughter shifting from chubby-cheeked giggles into long legs and frowns. She watched her, neither jealous nor proud – but rather amazed, in awe, and fearful for her. Fearful of what awaited outside the front door, inside the door of bars or on the backseat of a hatchback, or the words that could cut her when she dared to open her mouth with the wrong answer, don't you dare, don't you dare – or by being alive and simply glorious.

Alive, alive, alive.

So she hobbled along, bound in triple-cooked grief – wrapped tight by it all. Trying to hide and taking up too much space all at once. Until this became her. Until she was this. A mother without a child. A child without a mother. A woman without. A without woman weighed down and too fat and too old and too other and padded and round and invisible.

But taking up far too much space.

Then, it happened. She began to pick away at the edges of this cocoon. It was old and frayed, and perhaps it no longer fit. She scratched and scraped and found a sense of relief, and so she peeled away. Satisfying. She lifted off the layers of names and titles and obligations and loss until she found herself again, beneath. And then she rubbed the tufts that remained, the gossamer thin obligations you could hardly see, but they were there. She knew they were there.

Staggering like a fawn, she blinked and took her steps into the world.

So what if they called it a crisis? She did not care. She called it a resurrection.

Twenty-two

Blossom

(Second Place, Flash500, Q1 2022)

It was to be a hard winter, she said. The apple skins were thick as hide. Berries pocked the bushes in shades of purple and puce. These were the signs. How she knew.

She explained it to me in her slow and steady song, and I listened and watched, transfixed, while she harvested the witch hazel. She shook the scented white speckles, released a cloud of perfume – and smiled as I staggered from its force.

She showed me how to crush the bark and release the healing balm. We steeped it in water, doused a cloth, dabbed and daubed my skin to rise the cold prickle where it worked. My skin shone, pale.

I was alive.

"Iridescent," she said, "You are moondust." And she kissed my hands, my cheeks, and laughed at the contrast with her candied arms, her burnished chest.

That winter, she showed me many things.

We tiptoed alongside hedgerows, scurried and skipped in woods until deeper we went. Deeper. We explored the depths of the forest: sweet violet, Jack-By-the-Hedge. And we hid and lay with the God of Thunder under the powerful oak.

"You will remember this," she said. "You will always remember," as she tapped a plump linen bag of rosemary against my brow.

I believed her.

Deeper. Deeper still. Spring came, then summer started her soft knock against the door. I heard about the foxglove: 'goblin's finger'. How it came in the spring with a bob and bounce, even without the wind. "Fairy folk," she said. They scampered among the bells, wore petals like gloves, and danced, and jigged too quick for the naked eye. And they were mischievous, yes, but they helped the foxes to don the blooms in a necklace. Protection from the huntsmen – a charm to ward them off.

I picked at the blossom as she lay, dropping a pattern of pink across her chest, counting the bells where they bobbed and swayed. Wanting to keep her safe.

Her fingertips held a power. But they called it a curse, and by summer's peak, they had heard about our secrets. They whispered and hissed and broke them into pottery and eggshells. They tried to fashion us into a fragile thing – not the strength of the oak nor the force of the moon. And I knew they were coming. The huntsmen coming soon.

Time was running out.

Then, one day, as we lay, we could hear them. The men. The brutal stomp and yells as they came; the bells bobbed mournfully, and the tree's canopy stretched in a cloak, but we could not hide. She placed her naked arm around me, and I watched as a foxglove amulet fell – shrivelled, brown. I stared at her, desperately, into her – and she gazed back. She saw me.

"I love you," I said. "I will keep you safe."

"Always remember," was her only reply.

And we lay together, in those last few moments, amongst nature, amongst beauty – wearing petals like gloves, in the depths of the woods.

Twenty-three
The Plastic House

It's dark outside, but Dad hasn't mentioned bedtime. Maybe if I'm quiet, he won't notice me.

It must be the middle of the night.

The curtains are open, and the willow in the garden dances against the glass – a jumble of shadows and leaves. I don't want to look.

I'm sitting amongst a mound of scattered Lego. Red, yellow, white – plastic windows, bricks and bridges surround me like jewels and broken teeth. Dad's talking to someone on the phone.

"Should never have risked it," he's saying. His voice is half spit, half gravel. "I should never have let you come here."

Yesterday, I made a rocket. An escape ship. Today, I'm building a house. Square. Solid. I sift my hands through the cold plastic. I like the tinkle it makes, but I resist. Stop. Sshh.

"Your bloody locket," he says. "On the floor. How could you be so stupid? Or did you leave it on purpose?"

I can hear the sound of shrieks, tears, and fury down the phone. It's a woman, but it's not mum. Mum's away with Aunty Cathy. Home tomorrow.

"I don't bloody know what to think anymore! Trust you?" He snorts. "After this?"

He pulls a silver chain from his pocket. It's long and slinks through his fingers like a grass snake. I don't want to look. But I do. It glints in the lamplight, a silver locket on the end, round. A planet. Swinging from his hand, hanging low.

My Lego house is tall now. One door, four windows, and three figures lying next to me, ready. I've made a garden. I wish I could light the inside so they won't have to be in the dark. Scared. And there's a socket nearby – a lamp unplugged on the sideboard. But I don't risk it. Dad would see.

They'll have to be brave. Look out for each other.

"Phoebe. I know. I want that, too." His voice is soft leather now: warm and old and comforting. "But don't rush me. Just give me time… three months. Two…" The locket slips from his hand to the floor, almost where he found it earlier. When he had said that bad word. "Sorry. I… overreacted. Yes. And me? You trust me?"

I'm building the roof, but first, I take a plastic stick with a handle and hook and place it across from one wall to another. I can add a light there and hang it down so the little girl can see everything in the house. Everything that goes on.

"I love you, and I love the…" His voice drifts away into a deep velvet chuckle, muffled and quiet until I can't hear.

Finished. Just the three figures remain.

I take the little girl and her mother and place them on the grass outside the house. The dad remains at my feet, alone, and the little girl is staring through the window at the silver locket that now swings – like a chandelier from the ceiling – to illuminate their home.

Twenty-four

Wish

She blew out the candle. One germy puff and the flame was gone.

I wish I didn't feel so alone.

Through the wall, she could hear the neighbour's piano again. Perhaps she should ask for 'Happy Birthday.' Likely the only way she'd get to hear it this year.

Yes, Happy Bloody Birthday, Louise.

She pulled the candle from the cupcake and dropped it onto the coffee table, eating at least a third of the cake in one bite. The dry sponge hit the back of her throat, and the thick, sugary icing clogged her mouth, coating the roof and leaving a trail of sweet cement on her molars. It was both wonderful and hideous concurrently. She took another bite.

Her neighbour had moved on to a new piece. Undulating, in a minor key. She was too much of a heathen to know the name. But she recognised it. She pictured his fingers tracing on the keyboard, black and white blocks flicking up and down swiftly, dancing like a murmuration of starlings.

Louise closed her eyes. But tears found their way nonetheless.

Thirty-six. A one-bed flat, and no social life. Not even enough friends and family left for a phone call on her birthday. Louise looked about the space; grey, small, plain as it was. Three cards sat on the coffee table. She pictured Treena's birthday party six weeks earlier – the last time, in fact, that Louise had been out. There must have been thirty people there. Maybe fifty.

Treena had written a message on her Facebook wall that morning. *Happy Birthday, lovely lady. Hope you're spoilt rotten and having a blast! Xxx*

Louise took another bite of the cupcake, finishing it off.

***

He'd been playing for over half an hour now. On another day, perhaps it would have bothered her, but there was a strange comfort in it. She went over to the kitchen, finding scissors to tear open the cellophane of the bunch of flowers that sat in the sink. The flowers she had bought, herself. A riot of oranges and pinks. A strange, thick, musky scent. Somehow, the muffled sound of the keys through the wall was the perfect backdrop to this.

She picked them up, cradling them briefly in her left arm. She enjoyed the ephemeral weight against her skin as she held them close, on one side, as one might a puppy. A baby. A loved one. Then, she began to hack at the stems and pull away the lower leaves before placing them in a tall vase on the worktop.

He lived in Number 14. She'd seen the pianist: not often, but enough to nod and greet with platitudes, and once hold a parcel for him when a hassled delivery man thumped on her door. Older, slim, he always had a faint, inscrutable smile on his face. She wasn't sure if he was friendly or simply condescending. But he could play. Beautifully. She could hardly blame him for looking down on her when she looked up at him.

In Number 12, on the other side, there was an older man and woman. Louise thought they were called Mr and Mrs Francis, but it was too late to ask now, so they would forever be the couple at Number 12. She always saw them together. Stapled. But never talking. Never smiling. They nodded – one, two – when they saw her, then shuffled by. At least they had each other.

There was another young woman in 10 or 11. As in, truly young. In her twenties. Louise snorted aloud – no doubt she'd consider her decrepit. Last weekend, they had passed one another in the foyer of the flats – Louise returning home from the supermarket at 8.30 pm, Number 11 on her way out, silver dress pretty and impractical. No coat. Louise had smiled and said, 'Gorgeous shoes!' and Number 11 had looked down at Louise's feet in a reflex, where she wore plain, brown, Birkenstock sandals.

The woman – girl – had collected herself and smiled broadly. 'Impulse buy! I'll be carrying them by midnight.'

When I shall be sound asleep.

She could still hear her pianist playing softly, a gentle piece, but somehow, she wanted more. She strained to hear. How sad was she that this was the highlight of her day?

Louise walked down the short hallway of her flat and tentatively pulled open her front door. The music swelled and amplified now that she could experience it in stereo. There. That was better.

How must it feel to be so talented? No, so committed? Surely, he must never feel alone. If he did, he could turn and absorb himself in the wood and bone once more. He would always have that. And either way, he would not feel useless; never useless, practising and honing this incredible skill.

Louise listened, absorbing the tune from two directions where it almost seemed out of sync: one half brought to her through cotton wool, the other crisp and sharp. She thought she could hear the faint tap of the keys against the wood, miming a beat alongside the melody.

She had never stuck at anything in her life. Maybe that was it. The problem. The reason she was alone.

Number 9 didn't seem to have that issue. Handsome, hairy-faced, and short, he had a cacophony of guests several nights of the week. Was he Italian? Louise wasn't sure – avoiding conversation with him. Scared of illuminating the contrast in their lives. How on Earth does one get to be so popular?

But would she want that? She wasn't sure. It looked exhausting. It seemed he had to constantly laugh and smile and be coiffed with hair gel whilst clasping a phone.

The last time she had the misfortune to cross paths with him and his posse, there had been so many of them giggling and jiggling together that they couldn't all fit into the lift in one go. Louise was the first to take the stairs.

Was it helpful to dwell like this? Long-married couples, talented neighbours, the first flush of youth about her. And she, there, wedged in the middle. Stuck, as she had been for some time. No – she shook herself – no. There's no benefit in brooding.

So, what to do now? The cupcake was gone. The flowers unpacked. No plans. Would she have wine, perhaps? Drown her sorrows? But no, this seemed like another poor choice. She would have coffee. And perhaps another cake.

***

A small bag of shopping rocked against her leg as the lift doors closed. Milk, a carrot cake, biscuits, a magazine. A ready meal for one. Some bubble bath. That should last the night. It had been some time since she bought a magazine but figured this might prevent her from doomscrolling instead.

Louise pictured herself, a mug of coffee next to the bath, magazine pages dog-eared and soggy, bubbles dampening the jingle of the piano through the wall. At least she would have something to say when asked how she'd spent her birthday.

But then, who would ask?

As the lift reached the second floor, she felt the familiar lunge as it braked and almost doubled back, coming to a halt. She closed her eyes, wondering if her pianist would still be playing if there might be a mystery gift on the doorstep, whether the phone might ring, or if a message might appear on her phone screen. Perhaps.

She felt the breeze of the lift opening and took a step out, opening her eyes at the same time. Her flat was before her. The pianist to her right. And there, on either side, were the open doors of her neighbours. Like an unexpected Advent Calendar, welcoming in the sound of the music. Replicated. In union. Again and again.

Twenty-five

Bone

At a distance, the pond was beautiful. Flanked by ash and even a couple of picturesque willow, its vast, flat surface screamed serenity. Mallards bobbed in a cluster, and a couple of moorhens sat squat on the path, unbothered by the few people who sauntered by them. But as they approached, Lisa realised the water was cloudy and brown, a shopping trolley sunk in the mud beneath a shrub.

"It's glorious," he said, apparently oblivious to this intrusion by Tesco.

"A-huh."

"Thank you for agreeing to meet." He was walking with a little nervous bounce, balancing too much of his weight on the tip of his toes. His movement and formality were both equally irritating. He retained that vague smile on his face that he so often had, a mixture of friendliness and condescension. She vowed not to look his way again.

"No worries." The words came from a tense mouth, jaw clenched, teeth half-closed. Tinny and insincere. He didn't notice.

They walked along another fifty metres or so in silence. She could feel him beside her, a touch too close. Smell him: his usual soft spice infecting the fresh air. At least he'd showered and made an effort, she supposed. Not that she could say the same.

"Lisa," he said. Too loud. His volume was too loud for the public space, the breeze, her patience.

"Yes," she answered quietly to make a point. He turned towards her but continued to walk.

"None of this was planned, you know. It all just… happened. It was all a bloody stupid, messy mistake. I never would have intentionally hurt you." She didn't look at him, continuing to lock her eyes straight ahead, not even daring to glance at the water in case he met her eye somehow, in case he encroached on that, too.

"A mistake."

"Yes, that's all. I mean… not *all*. The things I've done, I'm not trying to diminish them. I just want you to know there's no master plan here. No evil genius. I'm just a twat who's cocked up."

"A mistake… the things you've done." She managed to crabwalk away from him gently to create distance. The spice faded, but his voice still cut through.

"Yes." He lifted his arms up and then dropped them heavily against his side in defeat, his expressive pianist's fingers fluttering as he did. He was no longer looking at her, thank God. No longer straining to catch her eye.

"Grammar was never your strong point."

He gave a half snort, indignant, irritated. "Grammar? What the hell has that got to do with anything."

"If it's *things* you've done, well, that's not *a mistake*, is it? It's lots of mistakes, one after another. A series of them. Several. Not single –"

"Well, I—"

"A serial mistaker."

He stopped. "Hang on, I'm not a serial… don't start exaggerating things. I know I've been stupid. I know I've cocked up. But we need to stick to the facts…"

Lisa carried on walking, enjoying the distance between them for a moment. Revelling in the space.

"The facts? I should say that the facts are that if someone takes the same action again and again, then that's not a mistake. It's a choice." She was surprised by how calm she was. How lucid. She walked on.

She couldn't hear his footsteps, and she wondered briefly if he had turned around. Turned back on himself to go back to the car. Lisa allowed herself to glance out towards the pond, knowing he would not be there. Knowing she was alone. A solitary black coot was on the water's edge nearby, ruffling as it splashed in the beige bath, white bill flashing bright against its black feathers. A piano.

Then he was jogging back to her. "Wait up." She stopped walking but didn't turn around. "I... You're right," he said.

She hadn't expected that.

"There must have been a degree of choice." He continued. "Of decision-making. Poor decision-making. It didn't feel like that, exactly. It felt like I was on a treadmill that was moving too fast. As if I wasn't in control of any of it."

Lisa nodded. But he was. He had ultimate control. Once more, she walked on.

He reached out and touched her arm. She slowed her pace. "I spent hours yesterday just playing," he said. "Playing pieces I would usually shun. Playing until my joints hurt and my ears throbbed. Because I couldn't process it. I couldn't shake the... the disquiet. But I never felt like I was in control or like I knew what I was doing. It didn't... But I am overwhelmed now by the guilt. The shame. It was my fault. All of it. I own it."

She stopped walking and placed one hand on his, looking up into his eyes for the first time. Gleaming, large, blinking too fast, his smile had dropped. She felt dizzy simply looking at him. She kept her hand atop his momentarily, then curled her fingers beneath his and peeled him away, feeling his ligaments flutter around the delicate bone. She could snap them. Easily.

"Please don't touch me," she said.

He took a step back. "Let's… let's just walk for a moment."

Lisa resumed her steady pace, stuffing her hands into her pockets. The air was dropping sharply as they approached dusk. She enjoyed the cold slap of it on her cheeks, the little dragon puffs in the air about her as she walked. She held him at his word. Silence.

It had seemed so exotic at first. A pianist. He lived alone in a flat packed with four-foot-tall plants, waxed and glossy in their perfection. He had painted one wall in a deep red – a striking contrast to the black shine of his baby grand. It took up so much floor space there was no room for a dining table, and they would perch at the breakfast bar eating Greek salad or homemade soup. He was a grown-up. A true grown-up. Grey-haired, independent, never seeming to falter in his actions or words.

They walked on, him sniffing periodically. At one point, he sneezed, laughing at the fierce sound. She could sense him glancing at her, but she didn't react. Instead, she reached down to pick up a long, thin branch, bleached white, with bark peeling. Skeletal. She planned to use it as a walking stick of sorts but found it too short, instead waving it awkwardly, as a wizard might a wand.

What did she wish for? What could she magic up?

They were approaching the car park again, their short, circular walk coming to an end.

He cleared his throat. "This walk was too short."

"Maybe," she replied. Maybe not.

"Do you want to… to walk around again? One more time?"

She looked up, frowning. "Don't you have to perform this evening?"

"No. Not tonight."

They faced one another. "Would you? Take a risk and go around once more?" He held out his hand to her.

"Take a risk?"

He smiled that inscrutable smile. She was still holding the white stick as a baton, flexing it up and down in the air between them.

"Give me your hand," she said with a smile.

Twenty-six
Green Bank, Research Notes*
(Jessica, Year 9)

- Green Bank, USA, has a population of 143. (141 in the 2020 census, but it seems two babies have been born since then).
- There's not much to do in Green Bank.
- Green Bank is the *National Radio Quiet Zone*. There's no phone signal or Wi-Fi. This avoids any interference for the *National Radio Astronomy Observatory* nearby.
- Everywhere should ban interference.
- Green Bank has an Arts Centre.
- Do you ever have a sensation of dropping as you fall asleep? Maybe it feels like that when you enter Green Bank. Perhaps you sense the drop and clutch your chest involuntarily. Falling down. Falling out.

- I have that sensation a lot these days.
- Green Bank is the *National Radio Quiet Zone*. It also has a steam railway.
- Sometimes, I turn my phone off for hours at a time. But it doesn't stop the talk. The chatter spits across my screen when it comes back on. Chuff-chuff. All that happens is that there's only half a conversation. And I'm the silent one. I am in the gap.
- But I can still see. I can still hear.
- Green Bank is the *National Radio Quiet Zone*. It attracts dozens of visitors each year. Some come because they believe they have *Electromagnetic Sensitivity*. Others, to get away from civilisation.
- *Electromagnetic Sensitivity* doesn't exist.
- (*Add additional notes about civilisation here.)
- And I wonder if it's truly quiet when there are still people around. If the lack of phones removes the chatter or if they're still thinking the same thoughts and saying the same things, just in a different way. In a different place. Tap, tap, chuff, chuff, spitting black dots inside your brain.
- Green Bank is the *National Radio Quiet Zone*.
- I'd like to visit Green Bank.
- But I am worried that I would still see.
- I am scared that I would still hear.

*Inspired by the real location of Green Bank, a town where Wi-Fi is prohibited, as it borders on The **National Radio Astronomy Observatory.**

Twenty-seven

Red Head

(A modern retelling of the Welsh Legend of Gelert the Dog*)

Llewelyn slept in the chair. He had curled himself up as much as a man of his size could, and one foot was tucked under his right leg into crumpled clothes. He was bundled up. His woollen socks had slipped down, hollow-toed, revealing red leg hairs, shocking against his pale skin. His cheeks were pink. His mouth ajar.

Bethan clicked the door shut behind her with a push of the hip and shuffled the shopping bags into the kitchen. The glass doors were open, just a crack, letting in the summer breeze. She unpacked the contents haphazardly into the cupboards and kept a small stack of snacks out on the side, ready for later. Crisps, nuts, biscuits. An optimistic bag of apples.

They were unlikely to cook.

The house was warm and still. She moved carefully in the half-light, collecting muslin cloths, sticky rattles, a buttery bib. The bottle of milk next to Llewelyn was only half drunk. She picked it up, and as she did so, it struck her that the room was not just still; it was empty.

There was no dog.

She dropped the bottle, and it flipped and sprayed her husband, coming down with a surprisingly heavy thunk upon his shin. She was at the bottom of the stairs before he stirred.

"Gelert?" she called as she grabbed the bannister. "Gel?"

Her stomach fell, and was tumbling further with each step on the staircase.

"Gelert! Here, boy!"

She heard a snuffle as she rounded the corner at the top of the stairs.

Everything twisted – her breath, her head, her vision – as she spotted bloodied paw prints trailing from the baby's bedroom out into the landing and back again. No. A firework spray of red was above the skirting. A door ajar that should not be ajar.

Bethan tried to call. She tried to yell Llewelyn's name.

At the entrance to the nursery sat Gelert, small, scruffy, shaky. His tail began to twitch when he saw her. He was breathing deeply. Around the white fur at his jaw, an unmistakable smear of blood – and in one paw, a ripped tuft of short red hair.

Bethan dropped down to her knees before him. Her legs dissolving into the floor. She could not bring herself to look into the room, the Moses basket, the baby. As long as she did not see what was there, it did not exist. It was not true. Gelert moved awkwardly as if to come to her, and she swatted him away with her whole arm across his nose – swinging herself around to face the scene as she did so.

The lamp lay on the floor. The bedside table was askew. Books scattered, open and shut, as birds in flight.

Another tuft of red hair. Another splatter. The basket overturned. A white blanket turned crimson.

A generous slick of dark blood stained the carpet.

She curled in on herself and fell further down, her wailing drowning out the words that she could hear from Llewelyn, somewhere near, but not here. Only she was here, inside this space, inside this feeling. Trapped inside this feeling. She was boxed in. Alone.

She felt the tentative lick of the dog on the back of her neck. His warm, meaty breath huffed out in short bursts.

Obscene.

Bethan reached across, grabbed the nearest book and brought it down on Gelert's head. She felt the contact on his skin and how he did not move while she brought it down again. Action without thought. He staggered back and took himself from the room.

Then, the house was still again. Truly still.

Silence. Then her breath came in choked lumps as she tried to steady herself, both hands down on her knees, clutching on, pushing herself down into the ground. She felt as if she could fly away; stars around her, head light.

She did not move until she realised Llewelyn was beside her.

She turned to face him.

"I'm going to kill him," she stated. "Now."

But he was holding a fox in his arms, talking, almost shouting.

"Bethan," he cried. "Bethan, look. Look!"

It took her a moment to take in the scene. The fox was punctured around his neck, a gash in his throat, his milky eyes open. It was a peculiar sight, this creature. Out of place. Warm. Dead. For a moment, she could not process this scene.

She watched Llewelyn drop its body on the floor next to the basket. The red of the fox was harsh against the white.

Then he stepped toward the basket and flipped it over – to reveal their baby: their tiny, beautiful baby beneath. Perfect. Whole. Alive. Arms lifting, fingers splayed and curious, legs bicycling in the air.

One sock slipped down, hollow-toed.

And a perfect head of short, soft, red hair, shocking and brilliant against the pale sheets.

The tale of Gelert the dog, is a Welsh legend, where Llywelyn the Great returns from hunting to find his dog with a blood-smeared mouth – and his baby missing. The cradle is overturned, and it appears the dog has killed the child. Llywelyn raises his sword and kills Gelert. After the death, Llywelyn hears the cries of the baby, unharmed under the cradle – then notes a dead wolf, which had attacked the child and been killed by Gelert in a display of loyalty. Llewelyn is said never to have smiled again.

Twenty-eight

Dear Steve

Dear Steve,
  This is the hardest letter I've ever had to—
Good God, no.
Dear Steve,
  I'm taking a trip to clear my head. But don't worry – I'll be back.
Would she?
Dear Steve,
  You utter dick.
Dear Steve,
  I hate you. I hate you. I hate you.
She placed the pen next to the thick cream paper she'd bought, especially for the occasion. It had seemed important to have a good-quality page. To leave with

some dignity. Even if Basildon Bond was the closest she could get to that.

But her handwriting was a fierce scrawl, and she'd already scrunched up five sheets into meteorites of vitriol, now strewn across the floor.

She entered the kitchen and pulled the cork from the wine with a satisfying pop – yanking her arms apart like an archer. His Bordeaux. She didn't even like red wine, and it was only three p.m.

She downed it; poured another.

How had it come to this? He hadn't even had the good grace to do something imaginative. A big, sweaty stereotype, he'd bought too-tight jeans and gone galivanting in his new car with a younger woman.

She'd suspected for two weeks before Martha saw him: tongue down a woman's throat in the pub. Their local pub. No doubt he thought it safe because she didn't go out much anymore. Never mind that other people existed in the world. Like friends. Neighbours. Their own blasted children.

She winced, took a swig, and marched back into the dining room. However hard this letter was, she'd better hurry up.

Steve,

I don't know what to say. I don't have the words to explain how I feel.

This was true. Because she actually didn't know how she felt, so how could she express it? Humiliated, definitely angry, yes. But sad? Heartbroken? Those kinds of soft, blue-grey feelings were nebulous and just out of reach. She wasn't sure she'd ever be able to claim them as hers. Not really.

She sighed. Was this really a big deal? This bloody foolish behaviour – he couldn't be happy either, right?

She tried again.

I'm—

She heard the purr of the taxi outside, followed by one sharp toot. Damnit. No time for poetry now. This would be short and sweet.

She finished her drink and went towards the front door as she gathered her thoughts. Her keys weren't in the lock. Instinctively, she slid one hand into Steve's coat pocket – to be met by a box of Durex. Open. And those blue-grey feelings shifted further away.

The taxi tooted again.

She opened the door and ran out, her one small suitcase in hand, smiling apologetically. She dropped the bag at the driver's feet.

'Just a moment...' she called, turning back to finish the note.

Short.

Sweet.

Steve,

I'm leaving you!

She added three giant, messy kisses for good measure. Then she placed the granite stone down beside them, on the bonnet of his car, and admired her handiwork — before she turned on her heel and left.

Twenty-nine

Stay

Sometimes, it seemed like fifty years since the man with the white hair had left. Others, like yesterday.

I remembered how he'd make a nest of blankets and open arms on the sofa, and we'd sit together in the half-light. And occasionally, he shared his bacon.

This man, brown-haired, not white, had put me in a car. Something was wrong. Car journeys and tense voices spelt vets. Or that place with the concrete floor and angry cats that yowled like infant humans through the night.

There was sand on the seat, gritty, from the beach. Yesterday, when I had just started to trust him and his serious, sad smell, started to get used to his shiny kitchen with dry, expensive food.

No bacon.

My legs were stiff as a board today. I wasn't sure about the beach at first, but soon, I'd found myself dancing in the foam, chasing waves, filling my mouth until I had silt in the beans of my toes and cool water on my belly. And I felt alive.

Maybe I could stay here, I had thought. Maybe.

We arrived, and he lifted me out. I didn't help, dropping heavily in his arms, listening until he knocked on the door of a fancy shed with his elbow. A woman appeared, and a thick, perfumed smell hovered around her. The brown-haired man stood taller.

There was a strange bed with contraptions, liquids, and a brush. I didn't want to trust her. Logically, I shouldn't. But when the woman reached forward with her wide-open smile and took me so gently, her comfortable warmth was hard to fight. My tail swung in a pendulum.

She was a good one.

Behind me, the brown-haired man was speaking. I looked and saw a sparkle around him that wasn't there before. And he was bouncing on his toes. Grinning.

He agreed.

"A rescue," he said. "Had her two weeks. Thought she should settle before I got that matted hair off."

"Bless," she said.

I could feel the flutter of the woman's heart and smell the happiness between them. Was I staying here? Maybe I could stay.

"I took some leave… to settle her in. Thinking of extending it, to be honest."

"Is that easy?"

"Ha! No," he said. "I'm a doctor. Accident and Emergency. But… maybe it's time for a change. Anyway…" He ruffled my fur. He was different, changed somehow; I could feel it. And I could feel the strings between them. "I'll stop rabbiting. I'll leave you."

He stepped away. Her body tensed, her heart dropped, and the strings pulled taut as we turned towards the funny bed. I scrambled, panicked, scratching her arm. I couldn't help it; I had to. I was in a tangle, and he was leaving, and we both wanted him there. I knew she did. I did.

The woman cried out and put me down as he stepped forward.

The brown-haired man took her arm to examine the stripe I had left. Severe. Bold.

"Let me look at that," he said. "Maybe I could stay."

Thirty

Rainbow

You are there, by his shoulder, when he sits down at his desk. Cherub. You want to curl up and stay with him; he wants to brush you off. *Not now. No, please.*

You are salt in the face of the devil. Salt in an open wound.

There, again, before him: glittering, mesmerising, rising amongst a wall of elbows and suits in the boardroom. You come from nowhere – out of place – and then the pain is there. The pain. Throbbing and seeping as a ruptured vein.

It drives them back. Other men fall away like rotten teeth. Black holes in a chasm. Chipping, dipping, one by one. They can smell the loss of you, sense his failure.

He goes to the pub. You are there. You are there.

You float inside the glass he downs. Of course, you do. Amorphous. Translucent.

Unreal.

He swallows you and takes you home; he wants so much to take you home. He will be gentle. He will be kind. He will carry you like a wren's egg. Like the perfect, fragile thing you are.

He wants to share. He wants to give. And so he wraps his arms around her, and they dream of you together. *Maybe this time. This time, you will be.* They dream and talk and sow seeds and plans and nightmares and fears, but they will have you one day. They will wrap their arms around you, as well.

Rainbow. Child.

Curl up and stay for real, he says. *Curl up. Stay.*

Thirty-one

Luna

(Winner: Dean Writers' Zodiac Competition, 2022)

Luna pokes her head between the clouds, smiles softly. She is tucked below Orion's elbow, next to Eridanus. It is cosy there. Quiet.

Below, she sees Jess walking the streets again. Luna has followed her progress each night since she returned. There were weeks when Jess did not walk. She stayed away after it happened.

Luna pictured her alone, at home. Showering. Sore. She was glad to see her out again. Walking. Thinking. Free. This was her place. She was Leo, the lion. Fierce. Self-assured. It did not become her to hide away.

Luna squeezed her eyes and tugged, contracting the air. She pulled, in, out, a concertina, an accordion, until Jess walked the path she wanted for her – a safe one.

Jess walked into the only coffee shop left open to order a coffee thick with silt and sugar. She sat near the window, watching crisp packets dance on the tarmac, the occasional taxi whizz by aglow.

Luna was in a dream, pleased with this result. Happy to see Jess a little closer to herself once more. She allowed herself a rare moment of relaxation. She allowed the Earth to move as it wished.

But then she was lifted as a needle and thread. Yanked.

Two streets away, Khaled was being chased. Three young men, angry running shoes, smacking the streets in confident strides. Scorpio, Capricorn, Taurus at their worst. Khaled wore canvas footwear, no coat. He had nothing that they might want. Nothing. He was nothing. In three minutes' time, they would catch him.

Two minutes fifty seconds.

Luna could not bear it. She pictured his nose, crumpled as eggshells, as a soft-shelled crab. Cancer. She saw the footprint on his cheek. Desperate, impetuous, she scooped up an empty tin and rattled it against the cafe window. Jess looked up.

Two minutes twenty-one.

Luna smacked the tin against the window again until Jess came out to bin it, as she knew she would.

This was the moment Khaled rounded the corner, neck craned around to his assailants, to the goats, bulls, scorpions amongst men —one minute fifty-one seconds away. He almost careered into her. Even then, riddled with horror and anticipation, he apologised and staggered to avoid her. Khaled felt his left ankle turn and buckle as he did so. Luna winced for him. Prayed her plan would work.

Jess knew what was happening in an instant – saw the cold sweat on his bare arms, the terror in his eyes. She grabbed him, pulled him in through the door of the café, wordlessly. Took him deep into the coffee shop, to the stools up by the counter. Khaled limped, his panting descending into sobs, and as the three young men ran by the café, Luna forced herself to dim a little. To drop her shine.

They did not see him. They hurried on. They went into the depths of the dark and the night.

Luna was delighted; blew the clouds apart, throbbing and glowing with glee.

They sat and talked. It took him some time to snap away from the fear, but then Khaled told her stories of escape, of a journey peppered with vessels, danger, dreams. Jess listened, nodded, thought of her own bruises. Of hope.

And then, twenty minutes and forty-two seconds later, Khaled and Jess walked the streets home together. Their streets. Their home. Stars beneath stars swathed in the light of the moon.

ALSO BY
Dreena Collins

Short Fiction:

❖ Wish Bone

❖ Embers (and Other Stories)

❖ She Had Met Liars Before

❖ Taste (Six of the Best)

❖ Collected (The Complete Short Stories)

❖ Bird Wing (A Flash Fiction Collection)

❖ The Day I Nearly Drowned (Short Stories Vol. Two)

❖ The Blue Hour (Short Stories Vol. One)

Novels:

❖ And Then She Fell – a suspense novel

As Jane Harvey

(Contemporary light fiction)

- ❖ The Landlord of Hummingbird House (Book One)

- ❖ Buttercups in the Basement (Book Two)

- ❖ Searching for Sandra (a Novella)

- ❖ Christmas at Hummingbird House (a Short Story)

Available in all territories

And Then She Fell

Extract from Chapter 1

From close by came the sound of young people shouting joyously. Free. Their splashing enmeshed with the beat of the music. I recalled the pool with its faded, steep slides. A swim-up bar.

I had left it much later in the trip than I had planned, this visit back to The Palace Hotel. I was not so brave, after all.

As I walked up the slope towards the Reception, my stomach writhed, teeth clamped together, and all those other pangs and sensations in my flesh, my bones, came back in the places where they had sat the year before. When it happened.

Extraordinary.

The doors closed behind me, and the ferocious air-conditioning hit my skin. The lobby smelt salted and clean, just as it had last time. It was all as it had been.

The receptionist was new, however, and continued on the computer as I approached. She held one finger up to show me she knew I was there but didn't make eye contact. I wanted to scream at her. Shriek. But then she lifted her head – curly, dark – and beamed.

"Hello, madam. How can I help you?"

She spoke flawless English with hardly an accent.
"My name is Catherine Keely," I said. "My daughter died here last year."

Thank you for reading my book. If you have enjoyed it, please leave me a review. You have no idea the difference this can make.

www.ingramcontent.com/pod-product-compliance
Lightning Source LLC
Chambersburg PA
CBHW020914180626
46816CB00007BA/2390